Driven to the Edge

The big man lunged at him again, and caught a handful of Slocum's shirt. He felt it tighten and the shoulder seams pop from the grip of the big, work-hardened hand.

Try as he might, Slocum was growing weaker, scrabbling for his now-lost foothold . . . And he was two feet from falling off the cliff.

He had one chance. Now or never, Slocum, old boy, he told himself. He reached up at the growling, chuffing face, got a handful of jowly cheek meat, and pressed his thumb into the man's eye socket.

"Gaaah!" the big brute wailed and lessened his grip on Slocum's shirt enough that Slocum rolled out of the hold. He swung his body upward and drove his wounded leg right into the bent brute's shoulder. The man grunted and Slocum did it again. The moaning man lashed out, trying to grab hold of him, groping blindly, wildly for Slocum. Then his hand found Slocum's rifle and he snatched it up, still shaking his head from the eye gouging.

"Oh no, you don't," said Slocum through gritted teeth. He drove a fist straight at the man's nose and felt something inside it snap twice under his knuckles, then smear sideways into pulp. An immediate gush of blood, warm and foul, burst from the screaming man's face. Slocum followed it up with a boot heel to the middle of the man's mouth, and still he didn't let up. Slocum kept pushing, driving the big man backward. In his dazed condition, the man never noticed the cliff edge until it was far too late.

JAKE LOGAN

SLOCUM AND THE HELLFIRE HAREM

JOVE BOOKS, NEW YORK

THE BERKLEY PUBLISHING GROUP
Published by the Penguin Group
Penguin Group (USA) Inc.
375 Hudson Street, New York, New York 10014, USA
Penguin Group (Canada), 90 Eglinton Avenue East, Suite 700, Toronto, Ontario M4P 2Y3, Canada
(a division of Pearson Penguin Canada Inc.) • Penguin Books Ltd., 80 Strand, London WC2R 0RL,
England • Penguin Group Ireland, 25 St. Stephen's Green, Dublin 2, Ireland (a division of Penguin
Books Ltd.) • Penguin Group (Australia), 250 Camberwell Road, Camberwell, Victoria 3124, Australia
(a division of Pearson Australia Group Pty. Ltd.) • Penguin Books India Pvt. Ltd., 11 Community
Centre, Panchsheel Park, New Delhi—110 017, India • Penguin Group (NZ), 67 Apollo Drive,
Rosedale, Auckland 0632, New Zealand (a division of Pearson New Zealand Ltd.) • Penguin Books
(South Africa) (Pty.) Ltd., 24 Sturdee Avenue, Rosebank, Johannesburg 2196, South Africa

Penguin Books Ltd., Registered Offices: 80 Strand, London WC2R 0RL, England

This is a work of fiction. Names, characters, places, and incidents either are the product of the author's
imagination or are used fictitiously, and any resemblance to actual persons, living or dead, business
establishments, events, or locales is entirely coincidental.

SLOCUM AND THE HELLFIRE HAREM

A Jove Book / published by arrangement with the author

PUBLISHING HISTORY
Jove edition / December 2012

Copyright © 2012 by Penguin Group (USA) Inc.
Cover illustration by Sergio Giovine.

ISBN: 978-0-515-15122-0

JOVE®
Jove Books are published by The Berkley Publishing Group,
a division of Penguin Group (USA) Inc.,
375 Hudson Street, New York, New York 10014.
JOVE® is a registered trademark of Penguin Group (USA) Inc.
The "J" design is a trademark of Penguin Group (USA) Inc.

PRINTED IN THE UNITED STATES OF AMERICA

10 9 8 7 6 5 4 3 2 1

1

With a quick poke of a finger, John Slocum tipped his dusty, sweat-stained fawn hat back on his head and eyed the brimming glass of bourbon the barkeep was pouring him. It had been a long time, weeks, in fact, since he'd come to town, and just as long since he'd had a drink. Life on the Rocking D had kept him busy. Back in April, the ranch owner, Dez Monkton, had sent most of his cowboys and a thousand head north on a spring drive, which had left the ranch shorthanded for the summer season. And that was when Slocum had ridden in, ranging for work.

It was now July, and he'd been working at the Rocking D ever since. The pay was fair, the work was hard, most of the hands were decent to spend time with, and the food, cooked and served by Mrs. Monkton, was a cut above most grub shack fare. It was a good outfit, and part of him considered sticking there through the winter. But he was a far-ranging man, in part because he liked the freedom of traveling the wide-open spaces, stopping to gamble and drink, should his whim or his wallet allow. Yet overriding all that was the thought that he was a wanted man with the possibility of bounty hunters forever on his trail. And that was the thing that never allowed him to get too comfortable in any one place. He suspected that was the part that would win out in the end—it always did.

With a grim smile, Slocum raised the brimming glass to his mouth. He was looking forward to the drink about as much as he had been that bath, shave, and barbering he'd gotten when he rode into town a couple of hours before. Then he'd stopped off at Millie's Café for a hot meal of pot roast, potatoes, stewed tomatoes, buttered biscuits . . . and dessert served up the way Millie knew best.

Slocum had still been eating when she hustled on out the front door the only other customer in the place, a broke-down old miner who, from the looks of him, hadn't seen hide nor hair of a lode in a long time. But it hadn't mattered to Millie. She'd propped the CLOSED placard in the window and breezed by Slocum toward the back room.

"Dessert, John?" she'd said, eyeing him over her shoulder.

He'd gulped the last bites of spuds, gravy, and biscuit, followed them with a swig of coffee, then trailed her to the kitchen. If this turned out to be anything like the last time she'd served him dessert . . . He found her where he guessed he would—in the storeroom, wearing a smile, an apron, and nothing else. Somehow, between his table and the storeroom, she'd managed to shuck her dress and slip her apron back on.

"Ahem, I was told I might find dessert here . . . maybe pie?"

"Right this way, sir," she'd said with a smile and a beckoning finger.

As good as the pot roast and trimmings had been, that dessert proved to be the most memorable part of the meal, not in least part because of the tasty way Millie had served it up. Turned out that his sweet tooth had been mighty hard to satisfy, so he went ahead and had himself a second helping.

A half hour later, Millie had buttoned herself back into her dress and, with a last squeeze, had ushered Slocum to the back door. "I have to get busy prepping for the supper crowd," she said.

"But I'm hungry again," he'd said with what he hoped had been a suitably gaunt face.

She'd pushed him out the door. "You think you're hungry now, you come back later."

Now standing at the bar down the street, he recalled with a

smile what might well have been the best midday dessert ever offered to him—and he had every intention of dropping by the café near closing time. But first, he was about to follow up that fine dessert with a smooth bit of bourbon.

The amber-colored nectar had just touched his lips when a groan and a crash sounded from the doorway to his left. He shifted his gaze, along with everyone else in the place, in time to see the Rocking D foreman, Randolph "Hap" Roderick, crash through the batwing doors and drop in a heap to the barroom floor.

The thin older gent was called "Hap" because he always seemed to be smiling, no matter the difficulty or level of danger of the chore he'd been asked to perform, nor the foulness of the weather in which he had to do it. Yes sir, Hap was known as a happy man. It was a trait that Slocum envied and, in his own way, had tried to emulate as he worked alongside Hap at the Rocking D these past few months.

But Hap wasn't smiling today. Slocum slammed the untouched glass of whiskey on the bartop, spilling it. He dropped to the old cowboy's side, eased him onto his back as the saloon's occupants crowded around. Hap's vest flopped open; his blue-checked go-to-town dress shirt was a mess at the gut, clotted with blood and scorched fabric. It had been a close-in shot.

"Hap!" Slocum leaned close to the man's ashen face. "Hap! What happened? Who did this?"

"Oh, Slocum, good." The man smiled, though his eyes teared from the pain. "I was hoping to find you." Then his smile faded. "Tunk . . . Tunk Mueller . . ."

"What about him, Hap?" He looked up at the gawking onlookers. "Somebody get a doctor, for Pete's sake! And the sheriff!"

He heard footsteps and the batwing doors slap open. Slocum turned back to Hap. "What about Tunk, Hap? Did he do this to you?" Slocum already knew the answer. Of course it was Tunk.

Slocum didn't have much say in who Dez had hired, being a new hand himself, but he wished Monkton had not brought on Mueller. The man was a walking sack of trouble from the get-go, shirking his workload onto others, starting arguments and fistfights. But Hap, being the foreman and a decent man, was always trying to find the good in others. He urged Slocum to give Mueller the benefit of the doubt, and since the D had still been shorthanded, Slocum had gone along with it. Now he knew it had been a mistake. He should have trusted his own gut.

"Mueller . . . never thought he'd be a bad seed, John." Hap licked his lips and Slocum said, "Get him a beer, whiskey, something."

Hap smiled again, coughed. "I never touch the stuff, John. Water, though, I'd like a drink of cool water, if you could." The barkeep tended to the request.

Slocum worked to keep the man awake and coherent. "Are the Monktons all right?" Slocum knew the ranch was all but emptied out, being as it was the first proper day off the crew had had in weeks. "Hap, were the Monktons hurt, too?" The wounded man's eyelids flickered wide again.

"Getting myself duded up to come to town, I heard shots . . ." His lip quivered and he swallowed. "Seen Tunk coming out of the house carrying some of Mrs. Monkton's fancy flatware . . . Didn't make any sense." His eyes turned glassy and he gritted his teeth as some unseen pain wracked him deep inside.

Slocum touched Hap's forehead. "Hap? Stay with me here. Come on, Hap."

The wounded man's eyes focused again on Slocum. "Tried to stop him, tried to talk sense into him. I told him he wasn't a bad man, but he . . . just laughed at me, John. Told me I was a fool. Can you believe it? Man just gave up on himself. Then he shot me, John. He shot me and rode north. I have never been shot before, John."

The bartender returned with a short glass of water, but Slocum shook his head. Hap was beyond needing it.

Then Hap's eyes closed and his smile came back. Slocum bent low, and in a whisper, the older man said, "Don't you ever give up on yourself, John Slocum. You're a good man." Hap's head slumped to the side, and he knew no more. One of the hostesses inhaled in shock and turned away, sobbing. The big bartender stood holding the glass of water, sadness pulling at his thick features. Until the doctor and the sheriff pushed their way in to Hap's side, no one said anything.

And then all hell broke loose.

2

Slocum bolted from the Lucky Stiff Saloon. As he mounted his Appaloosa, standing hipshot at the rail out front, he saw Hap Roderick's old buckskin, Sammy, head drooped as if he knew what had happened. Blood smeared Hap's saddle.

As Slocum booted his horse into a hard gallop out of town, he tried not to think of his friend as a dead man. Surely Tunk hadn't hurt the Monktons, too? Maybe the shots Hap had heard were just harmless warning rounds intended to scare them. But Slocum knew that the warning bells pealing in his head weren't lying to him. For once, though, he was desperate to prove his instincts wrong. Maybe it had all been a mistake—maybe the doc could revive Hap.

Stop it, you damn fool, he told himself. Hap's dead and you'll be the first back to the ranch and you'll find the Monktons dead, too. And for what? He was sure Tunk Mueller had hoped to find a safe filled with bank notes, gold coins, and all manner of valuable jewelry. But the truth was that most ranchers lived from the proceeds of one drive to the next, and limped along as best they could, scratching out a living.

Didn't Tunk know that the Monktons barely had two pennies to rub together? At least, not until the drive's boss, one of Monkton's friends from a neighboring ranch, returned with whatever the Rocking D's earnings would be after they sold the cattle in Ogallala. And even then, they would be lucky if they came out with enough to scrape through another year, and then they'd do it all over again.

It made it even worse that they were good people, kind-hearted folks who had been on their place since they'd been a young couple. Raised and lost three children there, all to childhood diseases, and all buried in a plot on a knoll behind the house, one tall pine shading the three white wooden crosses.

Slocum made it back to the Rocking D in half an hour. The little ranch house's front door was open, not a good sign. He rode right up to the front steps, shouting even before he dismounted. "Mrs. Monkton? Dez? You home? Anybody here?"

He dashed up the steps and pushed the door wide, stopping in his tracks, his gut tightening and a feeling of cold overcoming him. Laid out on the bare wood floor before him was Dez Monkton, belly down and bleeding, arms outstretched and facing the kitchen at the rear of the house, as if he were crawling toward it. And facing him, as if crawling forward from the kitchen, lay Mrs. Monkton, also amid a spreading pool of her own blood. Their outstretched hands still groped a foot apart by the time they'd succumbed. He gritted his teeth and checked each of them on the neck for any sign of a pulse, but found none, their warmth already fading.

Slocum stood still, his hands clenched into fists at his side, his breath hitched in his throat. He'd taken lives when given no other option; he'd seen many people die, on the battlefield, in accidents on cattle drives, and in fair fights when both sides were on equal footing. But it was the murders, brutal, senseless murders, most always committed for greed, for want of what someone else had—even if they didn't really have it—that gnawed the harshest at Slocum. Murderers were the lowest of the low, a step below men who abused women and children. And Slocum had no tolerance for any of them.

He turned from the grisly scene, and walked onto the porch. Soon he heard hooves pounding and looked up to see a dozen riders headed toward the ranch, dust clouding about them. They were led by Sheriff Brolinski.

"Slocum!" he reined up and dismounted. "Are they . . ."

Slocum slowly shook his head, and that one gesture told them all just what they didn't want to hear.

The sheriff stepped into the front room and took off his hat. He looked on the scene for himself, then stepped back out onto the porch. "Rollie," he said, working his hat brim with fingers unaccustomed to helplessness. "Ride on back to town, fetch Delbert and his wagon, tell his son to make a couple of coffins. And send some women out here. You know which ones, Mrs. Monkton's friends."

"Hold up a second there, Rollie," Slocum interrupted. "Can I make a suggestion, Sheriff?"

"Sure, Slocum. Sure."

"Bury Mr. and Mrs. Monkton together in one box. I never saw a couple so devoted to each other. From the looks of things in there, they wanted to be together. And maybe bury Hap with them on the knoll out back in the family plot, too. From what I've heard, he'd been with them a long time."

Several of the gathered men murmured their assent, and the sheriff nodded, "That's true, that's true. Sound thinking, Slocum. We'll see to it." He turned again to the man waiting on horseback. "Rollie, bring ol' Hap back here to his home, tell Delbert to bring his undertakin' equipment on out here."

Rollie nodded, booted his buckskin into a gallop, and headed for town.

"I reckon we'll hold a service tomorrow," said the sheriff. "Right now, I need a few deputies. Who's up for helping me bring in that murdering Tunk Mueller?"

To a man, the group shouted approval. The sheriff turned to Slocum. "How 'bout you, Slocum?"

"I'm going for him, but I ride alone. No offense, but I've tracked men before and I can make better time on my own. And I will not give up."

"You saying we'd give up and go home?" A bald man tending toward fat stepped forward. "The Monktons were our friends, too, you know. Longer than you knew them!"

Slocum shook his head. "I'm not arguing that. But you all have families and a service to hold for three good people."

Slocum stepped down off the porch. "I'm not saying don't go. I'm saying don't feel bad when you feel you have to come back home." He snatched up the Appaloosa's reins. "Me, I have no home. But I do have a killer to catch, and I will catch him—if it takes a month of Sundays. You have my word on it. Now I have to go. Mueller's trail is getting colder by the second."

It took him five minutes to gather his traps, scare up leftover biscuits, a loaf of bread, a slab of canvas-wrapped bacon, a sack of Arbuckles, and a handful of dried apples, all from the cook shack. He filled his canteen, let the Appaloosa drink, then rode over to the men still gathered in front of the house. They didn't seem to know what to do while they waited for the folks from town.

Finally, the sheriff adjusted his hat and squinted up at him. "I daresay there will be a reward, Slocum."

Slocum shook his head and looked toward the house. "I don't want it. Use it for something they would have wanted done with it." He fixed the sheriff with a steely glare. "But you make damn sure that the poster says 'Dead or Alive,' because I'm not making any promises about Tunk Mueller's condition when I drag that murdering bastard back here."

He nodded to them once, then booted the Appaloosa into a trot. The group of sullen men stood silent, watching the tall, rawboned cowboy, nearly a stranger to them, ride northward, the direction they'd heard Hap say the killer had gone.

Yes, he was as much a stranger to them as Mueller had been, but somehow they knew they could trust him to find Mueller, this man named John Slocum.

3

He knew he'd been on the man's trail, but for the life of him, he couldn't get Mueller in sight. He always seemed to be a day behind, no matter how hard he pushed. But by the sixth day out, judging from the sign, tracks, and the steaming remains of both horse and campfire, Slocum felt sure he was closing the gap. It was possible that Tunk had begun to relax his vigilance, thinking that perhaps no one had followed after his misdeed. By the time Slocum made it to the little Nevada town of Slaterville, he was feeling more optimistic than he had in days. He dismounted in front of the sheriff's office and roused a napping young man wearing a badge.

"Sorry to disturb you, Deputy." He stepped inside, extended his hand. "I'm John Slocum. Do you mind if I look through your dodgers?"

"No, help yourself," said the young man, stretching and yawning. "Fact is, I was about to fix myself a cup of coffee. You want one?"

"Thanks," said Slocum, dragging the stack of wanted sheets toward him. "Don't mind if I do."

The deputy set a tin cup of steaming coffee in front of him. "You a bounty man?"

"Not really, but I'm on the trail of a man who killed

10

three friends of mine little more than a week ago, down Arizona way."

The young man gulped, his eyes widened. "A killer?" He looked over his shoulder out the window, as if the man might be peeking in at him. "You think he's here, in Slaterville?"

"Well, I don't know where he is." Slocum sipped his coffee. "But I believe he at least made it this far in the last day or so. Goes by the name of Tunk Mueller. Could be an alias, but at the least I'd guess his first name is a nickname and not his given name."

"What's he look like?"

"Not tall, maybe half a head shorter than me. Sandy hair, could use a barbering. Brown felt hat, ragged band, not one for regular shaving, has a smart mouth on him. And he rides a dun mare. At least that's what he stole from the ranch, near as I could tell." He eyed the kid, whose eyes had widened again. "You've seen him, then?"

"Yes sir, I believe I have. A day back, as you say." He glanced over his shoulder again. "Sheriff's away, so I been tending to things here." He leaned closer and lowered his voice. "Only I ain't had to deal with anything more than the odd drunk cowhand of a Saturday evening, if you catch my meaning."

Slocum nodded. "I understand. But you wear that badge, you're in line for whatever comes your way, good, bad, or indecent."

"I know it, I know it. My mama is forever telling me to quit it while I'm ahead, but I just can't leave the sheriff in the lurch like that. Besides," he said, grinning again, "I kind of like it."

"It gets in the blood. Just be sure you don't spill your own. Now this Tunk Mueller, he make any waves, do anything while he was in town?"

The kid scrunched his cheeks in thought. "He visited the saloon, but hell, everybody does that." He snapped his fingers. "I know, it was odd. He swapped some stuff for food at Orton's Store."

"What sort of stuff?"

"Things a man didn't normally carry, forks and spoons and the like. Good stuff, too, at least that's what Mrs. Orton said."

"These Ortons, they good people?"

"Oh yeah, salt of the earth."

"Good. Thanks, kid. I mean, Deputy." He extended his hand.

As they shook, the deputy said, "Oh, it's all right. I know I'm young looking. But I'll be eighteen next year . . . or so."

"Well, you've been helpful. I have to visit the store myself to stock up for the trail." He stopped in the doorway. "Deputy, do me a favor. I doubt he will, but if this Mueller should come back through here . . ."

The kid put his hand on his side arm. "Don't worry, I know what to do."

"No," said Slocum. "Don't do that. Just let him go. He's a rattler. You poke him and he'll bite. You leave that killer alone. Let the sheriff handle him."

"Okay, Mr. Slocum. All right."

"Thanks. Be seeing you." Slocum walked the Appaloosa to the store across the street.

As he pushed his way in through the door, a brass bell tinkled overhead and a thin older man, bald and with a close-trimmed beard and spectacles, glanced up from behind the counter. "Hello there, what can I do for you?"

Slocum nodded and glanced around. It was a full store, lots of goods hanging from beams, stacked on the floor, a cracker barrel half-full near the potbelly stove, and a decent assortment of canned goods lining shelves behind the counter.

"You'd be Mr. Orton?"

"That I would. I know you?" The man looked at Slocum over his spectacles.

"No, the deputy sent me over."

"Oh, Jeff's a good boy. A bit keen, especially when the sheriff's out of town. But a good boy."

"Yes, he seems it. He mentioned a stranger came through only a day or so ago, sold you some flatware?"

Orton straightened, one eye narrowed. "Yes, what of it?"

"Well, the flatware belonged to a woman who was murdered."

"Oh dear."

Slocum and Orton both looked up to see an older lady with a hand to her mouth. She was short and not thin, but dressed well and wearing an apron.

"Maudie, I didn't see you there." Orton turned to Slocum, "My wife, Mr., ah . . ."

"I'm Slocum, John Slocum." He held out his hand to the merchant. "About the flatware, ma'am."

"I'll handle this, Maudie." Orton put both hands flat on the glass-topped display case.

"Oh, Horace, don't get yourself all worked up. Let's hear what the man has to say."

Slocum smiled at them both. "From your reactions, I'd say that you have, or had, the flatware. As I was saying, it belongs to a woman and her husband, of my acquaintance. They were murdered by the man who sold it to you."

"Oh dear!"

"Maudie, you said that already." Orton still eyed Slocum as if he were undecided about him.

"They were ranch owners down in Arizona. I worked for them. He also killed our foreman. I've been tracking him the better part of a week now. His name's Tunk Mueller—at least that's what we know him by. Not that it matters. I'll catch up to him soon."

"The silverware. It . . . Horace let me buy it from the man." Mrs. Orton looked down at her rough, red hands.

She'd probably been doing laundry, thought Slocum. Lye soap was rough on the hands.

"There weren't many pieces, eleven in all. I thought it odd that he had them in the first place, and those that he did have made up an odd number, not really a set." She looked at her husband. "Enough for two people to use." She looked at Slocum. "If I had known, Mr. Slocum, I never would have bought them from him, never would have helped him that way. But they were so fine, such pretty pieces. Something we could never afford."

"Maudie . . ."

"I understand, ma'am." Slocum turned his hat in his hands.

"To my knowledge, they didn't have any living relations, so it's possible no one would miss the pieces. I'd be happy to find out for you once I get back to Arizona."

"I'll get them." Mrs. Orton headed back toward what Slocum assumed was their living quarters at the back of the store.

"No, please. I have hard riding ahead. It would be better if you held on to them for the time being."

"I could never think of them the same way again." She didn't look at him.

"If you knew Mrs. Monkton, ma'am, you'd know she'd probably be pleased that you're so fond of her things."

"That was her name? Monkton?"

"Yes, ma'am. Why, does that mean anything to you?"

"No, not really. But it explains the engraved 'M' on the pieces."

"I see. Well, if it helps any, they didn't have much, but they were fine people, very kind." Slocum looked at Mr. Orton. "You don't happen to know anything else about Mueller? Anything that might help me? Maybe which direction he headed?"

The merchant scratched his beard in thought. "Well, he definitely left town via the north road. I thought that odd because not many folks do that. I happen to have seen him because I was out back . . . heading to the privy, when I saw him ride off. Hard to miss—bright red shirt riding northward."

"Why don't folks head north from here?"

"Oh, that old road is seldom traveled. There are easier routes to get to other places, California, Oregon. Most folks travel west or east or south. The north road leads through what we call God's Gulch."

"Some of you do," said Mrs. Orton. "I don't hold with speaking such sacrilege."

Orton shot Slocum a wearied look. "It's because of Old Man Tinker. He's about the only one out there now. Not a bad valley for farming, but there are easier plots to be had. I suspect the man likes his privacy."

"He alone, this Tinker?"

"Land sakes, no," said Mrs. Orton, setting three mugs on the counter and pouring coffee from a pot on the woodstove.

Slocum could tell they were leading up to something, but he started to get that jittery feeling. He had to get his supplies and get out of there. He suspected he'd gotten all the useful information from them he was going to get; the rest of it was shaping up to be a gossip session. But he took the offered cup of coffee and was surprised at how good it tasted. They were nothing if not a coffee-offering bunch in Slaterville.

"Tinker's a Bible-thumper from way back. Real brimstone type. We don't see him much, but when we do, you can be sure a trail of angry people and arguments dog him until he leaves town. He's just one of them fellas who can't leave well enough alone, accuses everyone of being in league with the devil. Devil this and devil that. Been out there for a couple of decades now, scratching out a living with his brood." Mr. Orton sipped.

"Hmm, some brood. They say"—Mrs. Orton leaned in and lowered her voice—"that he's . . . well . . . not a very good husband, and an even worse father. If you know what I mean." Her eyebrows rose.

Slocum didn't really know what she meant, but he didn't have time to figure it out. "I hate to be rude, but Mueller's getting further away from me with each minute. I would like to lay in some supplies for the trail."

He recited his order of coffee, jerky, flour, and an extra box of cartridges. And when it came time to settle up, the Ortons didn't want him to pay. "I can't do that, folks. It's very kind of you, but it wouldn't be right."

Horace Orton looked pained but didn't offer up a total. Slocum smiled and said, "I'll need a tally, Mr. Orton."

"All right then, make it two dollars."

Slocum knew it was at least double that, but he also didn't want to offend them, so he set three dollars on the counter, scooped up his supplies, and nodded to them. "Ma'am, Mr. Orton. I appreciate your help. And with luck, I'll be back through here before too long, with Mueller in tow."

Out on the street, he wedged the goods into his saddlebags. As he watered the Appaloosa, the young deputy came running across the street. "Mr. Slocum! Hey, Mr. Slocum."

Slocum glanced at the three other folks out and about on

the main street of Slaterville, and groaned. What now? He'd never get out of this town.

"Boy, am I glad you're still here." He handed Slocum an old, dog-eared dodger with a crude drawing on it. "I got to thinking about that Mueller fellow and something told me to go back through the old posters. We keep them in a different drawer. I only showed you the most recent. Anyway, I think this is him." The kid tapped the paper.

"Says here that his name is Thomas Miller and that he's a known murderer and thief, things I already know." Slocum glanced at the kid. "And this drawing's so bad it could be anyone." He did notice there was a bounty on the man from El Paso for $500.

But the kid was still smiling. "Turn it over." He nodded at the paper.

Slocum did and in an old hand, angled across the top left corner, it read, "AKA Tunk." Well now, that was something. "Good police work, Deputy. Mind if I keep this?"

The youth, now beaming from the compliment, said, "It's yours. I already wrote down the particulars for the sheriff."

Slocum mounted up. "I appreciate this, Deputy. I have a feeling it'll prove very helpful." How, he wasn't sure, but he wanted the kid to know he'd done well. "Time to go. Tell the sheriff everything I told you so there are no surprises when I come back through. And if I don't, well, you'll know why."

The face on the paper looked like a poorly drawn sketch of a sketch, would not look out of place on a cave wall. But it gave him slightly more information about the killer—and knowing that the man had a history of criminal behavior behind him only served to keep Slocum focused on the task at hand. He tucked the dog-eared, oft-folded dodger into his saddlebag.

He touched his hat brim and urged the Appaloosa into a loose trot. At the end of Slaterville's Main Street, he reined the horse northward. And within a mile, the roadway narrowed. Within three miles, it narrowed further at times from the inward creep of scrubby bushes until it was scarcely wide enough for a man on horseback to ride through.

A long time ago, someone had carved a road through an often thickly treed route. Now the landscape to either side had grown over it, and to get northward would require constant vigilance and slow going, lest a horse break a leg in the uncertain terrain. So it was a sure bet that the intermittent tracks he'd been following were probably Mueller's.

Given that he was in unfamiliar territory and the terrain had proven to be unpredictable, even on the trail, Slocum decided to hold up and make camp. There was little chance of catching up with Mueller that night, or even the next day, unless Tunk's horse came up lame. No, he'd do best to lie low and hit the trail again early in the morning, before first light. He'd pushed the horse hard all week, and other than getting slowed up in Slaterville, he knew the beast could do with a night's rest—and so could he. And with fresh supplies, he figured to make biscuits, bacon, and coffee, a real trail feast. It being high summer, there was plenty of green growth for the Appaloosa to browse.

As he busied himself with what few camp chores were required, Slocum let his mind trail back to the Rocking D and the kindness of the Monktons and Hap. A sudden sneer curled his lip—he should have run off Mueller before he ever got hired. If he'd only known.

But that was the sad thing—Slocum felt he had known that Tunk Mueller had been a bad seed. Knew it from the moment Hap introduced him to the skeletal summer crew. A snapping sound pulled him from his reverie and Slocum spun, keeping low and cocking the Colt Navy even as he snaked it from the holster.

The Appaloosa looked up from the bushes, munching and looking at Slocum as if he were wondering why the man was so skittish. It resumed its feeding, happy to have stopped for the night.

Slocum saw the snapped branches the horse stood on and laughed at himself. If he'd bothered to think about it, Slocum knew that there was little chance of Mueller doing any riding back to investigate who was on his back trail. No, if Mueller knew what was good for him, he'd keep on riding northward. At least, thought Slocum, that's what I'd do.

In short order, he had a half pot of coffee on, and a small batch of biscuits and several slices of bacon in his trail pan, plus enough for a quick, cold breakfast in the morning. Later, after he'd eaten his fill, he stretched out under the clear evening sky.

4

The last thing John Slocum had expected to see the next day—or any day—was a line of naked men lashed tight to fence posts, sagged but still held upright, their sun-popped skin boiled cherry red, bare heads lolled. He reined up beside a raw knob of sandstone and eyed the peculiar scene on the roadside before him. From under his sweat-stained hat brim, his narrowed eyes scanned the tumbledown rocks to his left, but saw no sign of bushwhackers. Whoever did this had probably already moved on. Question was, why did they do it? And how long had these poor fools been this way? His first guess, of course, was that it had been Tunk Mueller who'd done this to them.

All but assuming they were dead men, Slocum kneed the Appaloosa forward at a walk. His right hand rested light upon his thigh, a half second from shucking the sheathed Colt Navy revolver. Caution was never something he could afford to live without, and certainly not while on the trail of a killer.

There had been a part of Slocum that hadn't wanted to take on the tracking job, but in the few seconds it had taken him to decide to go, he had determined that the world would surely be a better place without the likes of Tunk Mueller on the loose. And now here they both were, headed north through Nevada, into a valley that, from the looks of these poor sad cases, Mueller had most definitely been through.

As he approached the five trussed men, he noted that one was older, judging from his bald head fringed with unkempt white hair and long, bedraggled beard the color of storm clouds. He was the man in the center. Then his conversation with the Ortons back in Slaterville came back to him. Could it be this was Old Man Tinker—he thought that's what they called him— the crazy Bible-thumper? What did Orton call him, something about being beyond devout, something about brimstone? He wished now that he'd asked more about the old man and his family, if only so he knew just what he'd found here.

To each side of the old man were propped two other men, each looking younger, though three looked to be in their twenties, and the last man to Slocum's left was barely more than a boy, gangly and less haired than the grown men. Baldness seemed to be creeping up on the others, though their hair was darker than the dirty white mane on the older man in the center.

The men weren't fat, but they were a burly bunch, looked to Slocum as if they hadn't missed too many meals. Their sun-reddened bellies, legs, and arms had bubbled between too many rope wrappings. Whoever had done this had wanted to make sure the men weren't about to follow. But why not just kill them? Seemed an elaborate amount of work to get up to just to rob someone.

Hold on, Slocum, he told himself. You don't know that they were robbed, nor even if they're fully cooked yet. He reined up before them, a runnel of sweat tailed down his spine, reminding him how hot the day had turned. And as if to emphasize the point, one of the men groaned.

Slocum jumped down from the Appaloosa and wrapped the reins over a top rail. It had been the youngster who'd moaned. Slocum knelt before him, looked up at the sunburned and blistered face, lips, and forehead of the boy.

He gingerly lifted the boy's face. "Kid, hey, kid? You're going to be okay. Just hang in there." Slocum winced at what he said. No time for jokes, Slocum. This is anything but funny. His sheath knife made quick work of the hemp wrappings, and as he sawed through them, careful not to let the boy pitch forward, another moan arose from one of the other men. Then another. Soon, there was a regular chorus of groans rising from the half-dead men.

"Hang on, hang on, I can only tend one at a time." He talked to them as he cut the ropes, and lowered them each to a prone position on the hard-packed earth. Their backs hadn't fared any better than their fronts—all blistered and redder than any skin should be. The men's hides were steaming hot to the touch.

The old man was the last to moan, so he was the last Slocum cut free. They each sighed in a mix of relief and agony.

As he cut them down, he asked of no one in particular, "What happened here?" His question was met with moans. He tried a more humorous approach. "You don't get many visitors out this way, I take it. Good thing I came along."

Again, more moans. But then in a low, hoarse whisper, the old man said, "Another came by. Stared at us, then laughed. Took our own water for himself and his horse, none for us . . . robbed us then rode out, laughing. A devil man."

Slocum nodded, but this scrap of information startled him. It sounded like how Mueller would behave, yet he'd been sure this was Mueller's handiwork in the first place. He'd ask about this stranger later. Maybe he actually was the one who'd tied them up, and they were just confused. It seemed the logical explanation. And it would have been like Mueller to leave these men for whoever was tailing him to deal with, for Slocum had been assuming that Mueller felt he was being followed.

But that still didn't explain who'd done this. If it hadn't been Mueller, then who?

"Hang on there, men. I'll fetch water, then get you inside." Somehow, he thought. But just how he would accomplish the task, he had no idea. Slocum looked beyond the fence toward a decent-size ranch house, barn, and fenced crops that, despite the searing sun of this remote stretch of Nevada, appeared to be growing well. Must have a decent source of water, he thought.

In short order, he had fetched a bucket of cool water from a well to the side of the house, halfway to the barn. The place looked decently built, tight, and tidily kept. The men all had similar characteristics in build—big, burly, though the youngest was thinner, more like a boy not yet filled out. But they were all obviously related, bearded up though the older four they were. The beards, he guessed, probably helped protect their faces from further burns.

Their bodies were crisscrossed with welts from the ropes and puckered where the ropes had bit into them and forced their flesh to bubble up.

Once he got water drizzled onto their greedy lips—careful not to let them have too much too soon, lest they throw it all up again—Slocum turned his thoughts again to getting the men to the house. A travois, that's what he'd need, then he wouldn't have to heft these beefy lads even if he could find a wagon.

He ran back to the barn, kicked two rails free from the corral fence, and dragged them back to the front fence. The men were beginning to stir, trying to raise themselves up on their elbows, their heads wobbling, still dazed.

Slocum used the ropes he'd cut from them, and lashed together a half-assed rig using his own blanket roll. He began with the old man and worked his way through the five, from what he guessed was youngest to oldest. Before a half hour was up, he had the men transported to the house, saving the youngest for last. The youth surprised him by struggling to his feet with the assistance of the fence, and leaning on Slocum, he managed to walk the distance of several hundred feet to the ranch house. As soon as they reached the shade of the low front porch, the boy sighed.

Slocum spent the next hour fetching water, and with the help of mumbled directions, he found a tub of salve that from its stink appeared to be made of bear grease mixed with something that came out of the south end of a bear. But it seemed to do the trick. He was thankful that by then the men had recovered enough that they were able to smear it on themselves and help each other. Slocum wasn't opposed to helping his fellow man, but greasing up a bulky army of sunburned men had pushed the limits of his charitable efforts for the day.

"So, you fellas related?" said Slocum, knowing the answer, but hoping to get one of them to crack a smile. It didn't work.

Despite the fact that he'd saved their lives, they seemed angry, almost hostile in their looks toward him, as if he had somehow been responsible for their plight. He decided not to let them know he'd heard of them in town. Probably a sore subject, and from the looks of their raw, bubbled hides, they had enough to be crabby about.

"They're my boys," whispered the old man. "I am Rufus Tinker, the head of the family, and they are my sons."

Where are the women? Slocum wanted to ask, but again, held his tongue. It didn't seem the time for many questions.

As the minutes wore on, the rest of the men were able to talk, in croaking voices at first, then in less strained tones. As minutes turned to an hour, then two, they were also able to shuffle around the house, and soon had pulled on loose-fitting shirts and sagged long underwear. It seemed to make the men feel better to have covered themselves up in front of the stranger.

He didn't press them, but Slocum was curious about their story. It being late in the day, and since he was still unsure if they were fit to take care of themselves, he figured he'd stay the night in the barn. He turned the Appaloosa loose into the corral and helped himself to some of the hay. The barn sat curiously empty save for an old mule whose livelier days were long behind him. He now shuffled about his own paddock off the back of the barn in much the same manner as the burnt men inside the house.

Slocum set his gear in a heap against a wall inside the barn, a decent spot to stretch out for a few nighttime hours. He was frustrated, but there was nothing for it. If he attempted to keep on into dark, he could end up with an injured horse, afoot in the middle of a long way from nowhere. His only consolation was that Mueller would have to do the same.

He headed back to the house and found the men seated gingerly around a big kitchen table. They looked considerably better, given the short amount of time that had passed since he'd freed them. He also noticed, by the looks they shot one another, that these men were angry. And rightfully so, thought Slocum. They'd been robbed, lashed to a fence, and left to die. But something about them and their plight didn't sit right. And the warning bells that he'd felt jangling in the back of his head were gonging louder than ever now. In part because they seemed, as before, angry with him.

"How long ago did that other man come by? I ask because he is a killer and a thief, and I am tracking him. Have been since Arizona."

The old man's knobbed thumbs worked back and forth with force over the worn brown leather cover of a thick Bible. His lips worked in a frantic, trembling, soundless speech. Slocum found nothing odd in that. Plenty of folks had a Bible around, and especially given what these men had just been through, he figured they might find a bit of comfort in the Good Book. A memory came to him, unbidden, of his mother reading her Bible by lamplight. He shook it off and figured he needed some answers. Before he could speak, the old man mumbled something.

"Pardon me?" said Slocum.

"I say I don't know more about the devil you are chasing," said Tinker. "Except that he robbed us, took water from us. Never offered us none, nor helped us at all."

Slocum nodded, mentally adding to Mueller's list the crime of ignoring his fellow men in a time of dire need. Not just ignoring them, but laughing at them, robbing them, before riding on. "Do you have any idea who did this to you?" He gestured toward them, assuming they would know that he was referring to their scarlet bodies.

"It was devil-sent bandits who did this to us." The old man licked his lips and continued.

Everyone's a devil to this old man, thought Slocum.

Tinker continued. "Tied us up out yonder, took our horses, money, foodstuffs." The old man glanced at the other four, who sat around the kitchen table looking at their hands, at the tabletop, anywhere, it seemed to Slocum, but meeting the old man's hard gaze. "And they took our womenfolk."

That last bit surprised Slocum. "How many women?"

"Hah?"

"I said, how many women did they take?"

"Oh, the Good Lord seen fit to give us a woman each, except for Luke there." He indicated the youngest. "Be a few seasons more 'til he's ready to spread his seed so that he might add to our congregation and bring glory to God by putting more men in His service." As he spoke, the old man's voice quavered and rose in pitch. He seemed to be working himself up into a lather.

The young boy blushed a deeper crimson through the sunburn. The Ortons hadn't told Slocum that there were people other than the Tinker family out here. Maybe he'd misunderstood them. Or the men might well have sent away for brides, immigrant women from back East.

"And the young'uns," the old man continued. "I don't rightly recall how many we got now. Too many, I reckon, all girls as they are."

Slocum didn't respond to the comment, another in what was shaping up to be an odd prejudice by this man against women. He saw the other men trade glances. "How long ago were they taken?"

"Couple of days."

"You must be anxious to trail them. Do you have any other stock? Anything at all you can ride?"

The old man made a noncommittal noise.

"I've never been on this trail before, so I'm not sure how far the next town is, but when I get there, I'll let the law know—"

The old man slammed a fist down on the table, cutting Slocum off and showing surprising force considering his weakened state. "There will be no law involved in our affairs! The Good Lord has deemed it so!" He turned to the others around the table and looked them each in the eye. Reluctantly they met his gaze. "Are we not men? Are we not made in the image of the Lord?"

They murmured an assent, which apparently wasn't good enough, for he repeated his questions in a louder, tremulous voice, and the four younger men perked up, nodding and meeting his gaze. It was obvious to Slocum that they were in fear of the older man with the flowing white beard.

Then, just as abruptly, Tinker tuned to Slocum, fixed him with what Slocum assumed was supposed to be a fear-inducing, withering glare. "We will deal with this situation ourselves, is that clear to you . . . stranger?"

Stranger, thought Slocum. After I saved your God-fearing

backside? "Perfectly clear, forget I mentioned it." Slocum opened the front door. "And rest assured, I won't let the law know of your . . . predicament." He looked at each man, then touched his hat brim. "Good luck, boys."

Then he turned to leave, but leaned back in. "One more thing: What did that other man look like? The one who stopped and laughed at you . . . you know, the one who *didn't* stop to help you."

The old man stared at him through puffy, red-rimmed eyes. "Don't know. Couldn't see so well. Sun"—he closed his eyes and swallowed—"sun was bright." His eyes snapped open. "He carried the taint of a bad man about him. A bad, bad man. A devil man. The Lord will strike him down, rest assured. The Lord will have His way."

"You'll pardon me for asking, sir, but if you didn't see him, how do you know he wasn't one of the ones who did this to you and stole the women and children?"

The old man looked up at him, his brow creased and hooded, a scowl on his mouth. "It wasn't—I know what I know. We was robbed by devil-bandits, I tell you. Godless creatures." By the time he'd finished speaking, his hands were clenched atop the Bible, his head shook, and spittle flecked from his mouth.

Slocum regarded the sad family, then nodded once and left the house. He'd made up his mind that they didn't need any more tending by him, and he no longer wished to be around them. They were, as Orton had said, odd, especially the old man. He had crazy, angry eyes and a dangerous sway over his sons. It also occurred to Slocum that if they had no beast to ride, they might think his horse was ripe for the taking.

He had just about gotten the Appaloosa saddled when he heard a small cough behind him. He turned to see Luke, the youngest of the men, dressed in a white shirt, loose black trousers, and holding the wooden water pail.

"You headed to church, boy?" Slocum smiled, tried to show the lad it was meant as a joke, but it was obvious it wasn't taken that way.

"No, sir. I . . ." He looked back toward the house. "I should be fetching water."

"Hey, Luke," said Slocum. "What really happened here?"

The kid looked back to the house, then down at his bare red feet. "The . . . the womenfolk—"

The door slammed and the old man shuffled out onto the porch, wincing as he stepped. "Luke! The Lord God doesn't look with favor on those who can't control their own wagging tongues!"

The boy looked briefly at Slocum, "I'm sorry," he whispered. "The man who didn't help us . . . I think he was wearing a red shirt." Luke limped to the well and hauled up a bucket of water with his blistered hands, the effort paining him. He didn't look at Slocum again.

Slocum locked eyes with the old man, whose face was red with rage, the Bible clutched tight to his chest in his clawlike hands.

As he trotted out of the yard on the Appaloosa, Slocum passed the house, the father and his sons standing arrayed on the porch, in much the same configuration as when Slocum had found them strapped to the fence hours before. Then the old man stepped forward, shook the Bible in Slocum's direction, and said, "If you should see our womenfolks, you tell them the Lord is on our side!" He gestured to himself with the Bible, then to each side, indicating his boys. "You tell them we are coming for them. Mark my words, we are coming for them!"

How in the heck are you going to do that? thought Slocum. You have one broke-down old mule and no weapons, and are so sunburned you can't even move normally. He didn't say anything, just nodded his head, touched his hat brim, and rode on out, thinking that the old man didn't sound so much like someone who'd lost loved ones to bandits as a man bent on revenge.

He was a half mile down the road before he allowed himself to breathe a long, loud sigh of relief. The Appaloosa's ears twitched. "Boy, I have no idea what that was all about. But I am glad to be out of that den of serpents."

As if in response, the Appaloosa nickered, bobbed his head, and picked up an extra kick of speed. Slocum smiled, agreeing silently with the horse's urge to put distance between them and the crazy farm. Then his thoughts turned to his quarry. He knew for certain then that the man who had passed them by had to be Tunk Mueller. He was the only man in Nevada who could be that heartless.

"At least I know for certain that I'm still on the right trail," said Slocum, slipping the leather thong off the hammer of his Colt Navy, and resting his right hand loosely on the saddle horn, ready to snatch the pistol free.

Fat lot of good being on the right trail will do me when, no matter what I try, it seems I keep getting slowed down. First in Slaterville, then losing hours with the sunburnt Bible-thumpers. What next?

5

Rufus Tinker and his four sons watched the tall, wide-shouldered stranger ride out atop his handsome dappled horse. Soon enough, the loping pair rounded the rocky knob to the west and slipped from sight.

With the speed of a striking rattler, Tinker's raw red hand lashed outward and connected with the tender-skinned face of the thin youth beside him. The boy's head snapped to the side, his lanky body—more boy than man—followed suit, and he stumbled, sprawling in the dirt at the base of the house's broad front steps. His gasp resulted less from the shock of his father's blow than from the pain his sunburned skin felt on scraping against the boards and gravel.

"Get up and get your sorry self in the house, fix us food. God's work cannot be done on air and promises. The rest of you, to the barn and fields, right things around and make ready for our journey. We will leave tomorrow morning."

"Where are we going, Papa?" the oldest of the sons asked. Though he stood taller and broader than his father, he looked toward his feet when the old bearded man turned his red-rimmed, steely gaze on the man.

"We are going to hunt down those foul witches, those demon-spawned fiends who robbed our growing congregation

29

of its future! We will track them down and drag them back."
The old man warmed to his subject, and with outstretched
arms, his Bible clutched in one red hand, he turned his face
skyward.

"I have been through fire and flame, and I have lived to hear
the words of the Lord whispered in my ears, though they be
burned things, and my very heart festered and bubbled and
boiled in my chest from the heat of this devil's playground on
which we dwell, I heard His voice! And He said to me, 'Rufus
Tinker, as My sole instrument of goodness and righteousness
on Earth, I command you to track down them evildoing spawn,
though they may be fruited of your loins, and though you may
travel the earth in your quest, this I command you . . . and your
minions.' "

The old man glanced to either side at his sons, then again
looked skyward. "You will bring the thieving witches back under
your control. You will make them see the errors of their ways,
even though it will most assuredly mean all manner of beatings
and lashings and privations such as their pampered bodies and
minds ain't never known!' "

He stopped speaking with an abruptness that forced the four
sons to glance at him. For a long minute there was only silence.
The old man's eyes were closed and his raised arms began to
quiver, then shake with the effort of being held aloft.

Finally, Peter cleared his throat and, in a quiet voice, said,
"How will we get there, Papa?"

The old man lowered his arms. "I will ride the mule, our only
remaining beast of burden, and you four will walk alongside."

"Where will we get—"

"The Lord will provide! I have said all I aim to say. Shut
your foul mouths and get to work, lest I become convinced you
are in secret league with those devils from hell."

The three older sons winced with the sting of his words and
scurried off to their respective tasks in the fields and barn as
fast as their burnt bodies allowed.

Luke crouched low and walked around the old man. The
boy faced downward but his eyes skittered as he tried to keep
his glaring father in sight. But he didn't see the old man's boot.

It connected with the boy's backside and sent him sprawling into the front room of the house.

As he picked himself up, the old man's broad, lanky form filled the doorway. "You will don that creature's apron and fix us men good food, and fast, or you will feel the full weight of the wrath of the Lord's Right Hand on Earth!"

The boy nodded and backed toward the kitchen.

"What do you say to that?"

"Yes, sir."

"That is not what I expected to hear!" The old man advanced, his spadelike hands held before him like great red weapons, the Bible clutched in one.

Luke bent behind the broad knife-scarred worktable and said, "Yes, Papa. Anything you want. I'll make the food now. Please don't hit me!" He voice quivered as he begged, but it was no use. The old man was lathered, and set the Good Book down with reverence before advancing on the boy once again.

From out in the barn, the three older brothers exchanged quick, darting glances when they heard Luke's howls. None dared say a thing to one another, knowing that any one of them might tattle to their papa about the others, then all would feel the sting of his hands, his switch, his belts, his hardwood paddle. They all bore knotted scars on their heads, roped welts on their shoulders, on their backs, marks that would never heal—all from their father's anger.

But brought on, so they were told and so they came to believe, because they were in league with the devil—they were slothful and ignorant and useless. And they knew they were. They tried not to be, but they must be, because their father was the Lord's Right Hand and how could they doubt the will of God? Even if that Right Hand hurt like hell sometimes.

6

Tunk Mueller figured he was being followed by someone. Or would be at some point—if not for that El Paso mess, then surely for dispatching that cheap old Dez Monkton and his scrimy wife, not to mention that do-gooder foreman, Hap. What sort of a name was that for a man? Mueller chuckled to himself and booted the dun mare into a trot.

Damn horse was handsome, but a laggard. Should have known better than to steal a beast from the Rocking D. Everything there was too prissy for his taste. Take that Slocum, always butting in, making fights his business, making sure Mueller'd been working when he needed a rest.

"Best thing I ever done was leave that mess behind. Why, I—" Mueller cut short his latest speech to the horse. He'd heard something from up ahead. Sounded like . . . children shouting? "What in the world?" He slowed the horse and soon stopped it altogether. They stood like that for several minutes, facing forward and listening, the horse and its rider, ears perked toward the unmistakable sounds of kids playing and having a grand old time somewhere up ahead. Mueller had assumed that since the road had been all but empty of signs of human settlement—other than those boiled farmers strapped to the fence—his path wouldn't cross anyone else's.

"Hmm," he grunted, and urged the horse into a slow walk. Must be the tracks he'd been spotting now and again in the lane, from a wagon and other footprints. Could be they're camping up ahead. Or could be they live there. Either way, they might have food and, more important, desirables such as money and jewelry and liquor. Mueller guided the horse off-trail, up to the right.

He dismounted, tied his horse off to a sapling, and crept forward. As he approached the top of a slight rise, the sunken roofline of an old house, looking long abandoned, rose up into his view. He slipped off his sweaty, flop-brim hat, and crawled on his belly and peeked farther over the edge of the rocky outcropping. He saw a wagon parked behind the house, and nearby an old stable. And then he couldn't believe his eyes.

Must have been four or five women, most of them handsome, at least from a distance, and a whole clot of kids running around, shouting and screaming like piglets. They all looked to be girls, too. Mueller licked his lips. He sure could do with a woman. But it was the sudden thought that these women surely had menfolk somewhere close by that kept him from scrambling down the slope and treating them ladies to the wonders of Tunk Mueller.

And then he saw that all those women appeared to be carrying weapons. He turned around and slid down out of sight. His jaw dropped and his dirt-smeared hand went to the butt of his pistol. Surely it couldn't be as bad as all that? But then he thought he heard a branch snap not far away. What if the menfolk were close by? Maybe hunting up game for their families before moving on. Best cut your losses, Tunk, he told himself. Get while you can and pretend you never even saw them women.

Mueller managed to do half of that in the next few minutes—he got out of there without being seen, he hoped, by angry husbands, sons, brothers. He cut a wide circle around the place, headed northward off the road and toward high country, his destination anyway. He had hoped to find another town, rob a little of this and that to keep body and soul together until he made it to his brother's spread in Northern Cali, but since he was headed in that direction already, he told himself, why not keep on?

But for the next few hours, he could not forget what he had seen. What if they had been all just women, traveling alone with no men to protect them? What if they found they needed a man?

He even reined up once, sat his horse atop a treed ridge, and looked back southward toward the old road, then northward toward where he needed to head. He scratched his chin and made a deal with himself. "Tunk, my man," he said, one leg out of the stirrup and resting canted over the horse's neck. "You pitch yourself a camp down yonder in that stand of trees on the flat. Settle in there for a night, give this situation some thought. Maybe ride on back and watch them pretty things, see what sort of men they have with them."

He smiled and nodded to himself. "Ain't many men who can stop a bullet or two. I expect you ladies will have a chance to meet Tunk Mueller yet." He swung his leg back over the horse's neck and nudged the beast into a zigzagging path to the flat beyond the ridge.

7

Slocum slipped down off the Appaloosa, checked the tracks he'd been following. No easy way to tell if the freshest tracks were Mueller's, but they had to be. Unless the outlaw cut off the old trail and headed cross-country, these topmost tracks, the freshest, were Mueller's. But there were plenty of others, too, and they made tracking a bit confusing. If Slocum could believe what Tinker had said, then the wagon and other hoofprints were from the bandits who had made off with the Tinker women and children. But something about that old loon's story just didn't sound right.

He wanted to let it go, but as he traveled, he had found himself dwelling on the peculiar man, his boys, and the manner in which they'd been strung up against the fence, as if whoever did it intended to kill them, but had wanted to be long gone when the end came.

Now, crouched on the dusty trail, Slocum followed various prints back and forth, intrigued more than he needed to be. What harm could a couple more minutes be, he asked himself as he studied wide-ranging clusters of children's footprints. They were made by kids of different sizes; that was plain enough. But curiously, they were all over the place, not made by kids who were kept as prisoners. He would expect them to be tied in a wagon.

35

And the boot prints that he did see were smaller than a man's—
most likely they were made by women.

He mounted up and put in another few hours before he had
to knuckle under to the day's dying light. He made a light camp
just off the trail, kindled a fire small enough to make coffee and
fry bacon. He still had a couple biscuits from his last camp, so
when the bacon had cooked through enough to suit his hungry
belly—which wasn't very long—he folded them up and sand-
wiched them between the split halves of the biscuits. He ate them
too fast; they tasted so good he wished he had a half-dozen more.
He wiped his greasy fingers on his denims and made do with
another cup of hot black coffee, then lay back for a few hours of
sleep. As he sank into its wide-open arms, he thought again of
the curious sunburnt men, of their women and children. The last
thing he decided before he gave in fully to slumber was the possibility that those women hadn't been spirited away by bandits—
they'd run away. Sensible women, given what they were fleeing
from.

8

Slocum heard the steady pounding sound before he saw where it came from. It rang at times, the unmistakable clang of metal striking metal, as if a blacksmith's shop were just around the bend. Another house? Well, it looked like decent land, so it shouldn't surprise him that it would be settled. After all, the old Bible-thumper had done just that, and judging from his place, Slocum thought he'd been there a good long while. A couple of decades, Orton at the store had told him, not that Slocum cared.

He only wanted to make tracks in hopes of gaining on Mueller. About the only good thing that came out of the episode with the old man and his boys had been learning that it was likely Mueller who'd passed them by. Slocum supposed it should make him feel good that he'd at least had decency enough to stop and help the poor bastards.

He'd left the sunburned father and sons behind him a day before. He hadn't minded clearing out of there once he'd realized the old man was as crazy as a blind rat. Slocum also figured it wouldn't take them long to figure out that he had a decent horse and they had nothing but the old mule. He figured he'd done enough; the rest was up to them. The fact that their women were gone troubled Slocum, but from what he could tell by the old man's attitude, it bothered Slocum more than it did them. They seemed angry, but with the women, not the bandits.

Slocum shook his head, ticked with himself for still thinking about it. "Too odd by half," he muttered to himself. If the Appaloosa heard him, it didn't show it, but kept up his steady, determined pace.

Soon, he heard shouts from up ahead, random and unhurried, possibly the exuberant yelps of children playing. Kids? Way out here? But he didn't have time to follow up on that line of thought, for he heard the lever action on a rifle ratchet from the ledge to his left, and a low, hard voice shouted, "That's far enough, stranger!" It was a woman's voice.

By the time she'd reached the end of her declaration, Slocum had his Colt Navy drawn and had vaulted from his saddle on the right, keeping the horse between him and whoever it was who'd gotten the drop on him. He scanned the rocky knob, but saw nothing move. A handful of gravel bounced down the talus slope. His horse fidgeted and Slocum gripped his side of the saddle, pulled back on the reins, tried to steady the cantankerous beast. But it didn't work—the horse reared, whinnied, and bolted free from his hands. It continued down the road and disappeared at a gallop around the upcoming bend.

Slocum stood crouched in the lane for all of a half second, then dashed forward, crossing the lane and making for the base of the ledge. No shots followed him, so the shooter might have been bluffing, or she might also have her sights on him right now. He kept his back tight to the rock, and squinted upward. No face peered down at him, no shots pinged off the ledge.

He was about to shout, try to get a response to help him fix on a spot, when he had a better idea. He stepped slowly to his right and worked his way around the base. The small cliff stood sheer just above him for another dozen yards before tailing downward in a crumbled pile of rocky debris. It wasn't much, but it might be enough for him to climb up, maybe surprise whoever it was up there.

He kept on climbing, steady but not too slow. He had a potential killer to catch, after all. He still heard nothing from above, but he also noticed something else he didn't hear. The sound of ringing that had carried to him on the light breeze before. And the sound of the children shouting, too, had ceased. The Appaloosa had been seen, riderless, perhaps even caught. Slocum wasn't impressed with that beast at the moment. He had a sudden urge to shoot the thing in the temple and be done with it. But he knew he was thinking out of anger. The horse had only reacted in surprise, and so had he, for that matter.

He was almost to the top of the ledge knob, careful with each step to make sure he didn't dislodge any loose rock, when a woman appeared before him, backing toward him, not three feet away. Slocum paused, watched her for a moment. She wore a rough-spun shirt of natural color, dark trousers that looked too large about the waist, cinched up with rope, and her near-black hair had been pulled back and pinned atop her head, strands trailing from it as she stepped slowly backward. He couldn't help noticing she had a pretty and graceful neck.

"That's far enough, stranger," he said in a low voice, poking the pistol barrel between her shoulder blades. "Don't turn around, don't do anything but stand still and keep quiet."

Her breathing grew rapid and Slocum saw her head tremble, whether from fear or anger, he could not tell.

"Now, ease off and set that rifle down on the ground. Slow, slow, slow—and steady."

She did and he nodded, kept an eye on her and reached into her sight line to grab the rifle butt and slide it toward him. She lashed out sideways with a mule kick that he was half expecting. He stepped away from it mostly. She still managed a solid hit just below his shoulder before he used her own momentum against her. He stood fast, hefting her booted foot with him, and halfway to standing, pushed her toward the boulder.

She slammed against it, rolled off, and stood facing him, her cheek red from where it hit the rock, her bottom lip split and bleeding. And in her eyes—sparks of rage. Her nostrils flexed, and as she breathed, her pretty white teeth were set together hard. This was a tiger of a woman, he thought, half smiling as he watched her. They circled, Slocum careful to kick the rifle with him as he moved, just out of her reach.

"You . . . you're just like all the rest!" she growled at him.

"Rest of what?" said Slocum, circling and shoving the rifle away from her. He had no intention of shooting her, not just because she was a woman, but because there was something about her that seemed confused, protective of something. She didn't seem like a desperado or hard case. He couldn't put a finger on it, but as far as he knew, they'd never met. He had no idea who or what she was, so he was puzzled about why she could hate him.

"Men!" She spat the word as if it tasted foul.

So that was it—she was a man hater. Pity, he thought. She was a fine specimen of a woman. "Look, ma'am, I don't know what you have against . . . my kind, but I can tell you, I don't believe we've ever met and I certainly have never done anything to offend you—or worse, make you hate me. Even drunk, I'd recognize you, trust me."

Somehow, that seemed to almost stir the spark of a smile on her mouth. Still, she crouched, tensed on the balls of her feet, her hands raised before her, fingers curled statue-like as if ready to claw the air. But her eyes moved back and forth, back and forth across his face, taking him in with a long, constant glance, her ample chest heaving with deep breaths, her fury palpable.

He sensed she was about to make a move for him, some animal lunge. And then, not too far off, a child howled as if it had skinned its knee, and her aggressive pose softened as if someone had blown out the guttering flame on an oil lamp. Her gritted teeth, the warring emotions of excitement and anger that had formed her face into a hateful mask, subsided.

She straightened, and she turned her face toward the sound. "I have to go." She turned back and faced Slocum.

"You should come down to the house. You look hungry."

Slocum didn't move, kept the Colt Navy aimed at her chest.

In the distance, the child howled again. "I need to go," she said, an eyebrow arched at him.

"You drew down on me, lady, remember? Whatever is happening can wait a minute. Who are you? And why did you want to rip out my throat just a few seconds ago?"

She pursed her lips, her hands on her waist. "I'll need my rifle."

He sighed, realizing he wasn't going to get a thing out of her. Yet. "Nah, no way. Just get going, I'll follow."

Her face hardened and she gritted her teeth again.

"You don't really think I'm going to give you a weapon after all that?" He motioned with his head. "Now get going."

They made it down to the dirt road and had walked a few yards when she looked over her shoulder as she walked. "You like what you see?"

Slocum had to smile at her plain crazy ways. "Yeah," he said. "Mighty pretty . . . country."

She laughed, a throaty sound that Slocum found sexy.

He had no idea just what he was walking into, but he had to admit it had been an interesting few days. And this answered his question of earlier: What next? He was about to find out. He took his eyes off her backside long enough to see that they'd rounded that bend in the road. And he couldn't believe what he saw.

9

A teeming gaggle of children, all little girls from the looks of
them, bubbled and squirmed, shouting and chasing one another
in circles. Beyond them sat a small farmhouse, adobe in con-
struction, and missing half of its roof, the porch a sagging thing
at one end. Beyond that sat a corral and low, open-sided barn,
the wood siding curled and puckered through years in the sun.
And there stood the Appaloosa, hipshot, still saddled, and looking at ease, as if he were catching a few winks in the afternoon sun.

"Damn horse," said Slocum under his breath, though he was
relieved to see it hadn't abandoned him at what was shaping
up to be another nest of strange strangers.

As they approached, the group of six or more children, ranging in age from toddlers to just under eight years or so—it was
difficult for Slocum to guess with any certainty—swung their
heads toward them as if by instinct. Half of them, it seemed to
him, bolted toward the woman before him, shouting, "Mama!
Mama!"

"Ruth! Ruth, that you?" came a voice from the little house.
A stout woman seeming no taller than Slocum's rib cage shouted
from the porch, drying her hands on a much-used apron. "Where
have you been, girl?" Then she must have caught sight of Slo-

cum, because she visored a hand above her eyes and her voice
took on a sharp, growly edge. Had to be the wildcat woman's
mother. "Who in the blue blazes is that? A . . . *man*?"

The children by then had swarmed Ruth and she looked at
Slocum and said, loud enough for the old woman to hear her,
"Oh, he's a man, all right."

John Slocum had many times been the fond recipient of
amorous intention, as if he were being sized up for a roll in the
hay. And that's exactly the sort of look Ruth was giving him;
not for a second apparently did she consider the fact that it
seemed as if half the teeming mass of children about her legs
were anything to him but a distinct shock and letdown. And yet
that face of hers was a stunner, something bold and chiseled
about it, her dark eyebrows and full lips, between which a long
nose, slightly arched as if in pride, seemed to sniff at him of its
own accord.

Slocum looked back across the yard. The old woman had
retrieved a shotgun from somewhere. But that wasn't what
shocked him. Flanking the scowling old thing stood three more
women, two of them filled out so that even at this distance he
saw they were nearly a matched set, more women than girls, and
the third was a younger thing, barely into her teen years. Each
of the three new arrivals was armed.

"Oh my, what have you stumbled upon, sir?" said Ruth,
reading his mind and following up her comment with that same
throaty laugh that, despite the strange situation, stabbed him
deep in his groin.

He knew exactly what he'd stumbled upon. And it was what
Old Man Tinker called "his womenfolk." So here was his proof
that the bandits who supposedly took them were nonexistent,
and these women had fled the crazy man of their own free will.
That made some sense, considering how he'd heard Tinker run
down women, as if they were put on earth for breeding purposes.
Slocum would be the first to admit that spending time with
women could be a whole lot of fun, and had its own rewards. But
he'd also known far too many that were the equal or better of
many men ever to generalize about them or regard them as
somehow inferior.

And this lot was anything but, especially bristling with all that firepower. Slocum had no intention of approaching the house without keeping Ruth before him. It wasn't but a short while before that she'd been trying to ambush him. And he still didn't know why.

"My rifle, if you don't mind." She held out a strong, callused hand and beckoned with her fingers.

Downright demanding, thought Slocum. "As it happens," he said, careful not to point the muzzle of his pistol or the rifle toward the kids or the house. "I do mind. And no, I don't trust you."

The kids looked at him with a mixture of mistrust and confusion, but one little girl caught his own gaze and smiled, her red cheeks bunching high, before burying her face against Ruth's leg.

He had to smile. "Yours?"

"Not all of 'em." She looked at the kids, who'd begun to wander off, wrestling and shrieking and pushing one another. "Enough, though."

Where before she'd looked fiery and mischievous, now she just looked tired.

"What's say we try to talk your friends over there into putting down their weapons before I end up hurt. I have a long way to go and a short time to get there."

She nodded as they walked toward the house, but before she could reply, he said, "Which reminds me, you haven't seen any other men out this way, have you?"

The question stopped her in her tracks. "What . . . makes you ask that?"

Interesting, he thought. Given that the road was not too heavily traveled, he was beginning to wonder if he had lost Mueller's trail. Do have to wonder if these women and kids just might be the ones the bandits supposedly absconded with back at the old man's place. If so, he thought, they look fine and dandy, and that's as far as I care to take the matter.

"Because I am tracking a man," he said, choosing to keep the sunburned gang out of conversation for the time being.

"I believe he's wearing a red shirt, or was at one time. He's done some bad things, shouldn't be trusted." He nodded toward the gaggle of kids. "Especially not where kids and women are concerned." And once again, it was as if he'd flipped a switch.

She turned on him, her teeth set, that glint in her eyes, but nothing playful about it now. She poked a finger at him, all but ignoring the pistol in his hand and the rifle within swinging distance. "You got a lot of gall to say that to me, mister. I'll have you know we all can take care of ourselves just fine without the help of any menfolk."

"Yeah, well, you haven't run into Tunk Mueller."

Ruth turned her back on him and said, "Or maybe he ain't run into us."

Slocum could only nod. It appeared he'd stumbled into a nest of she-vipers and he didn't want to be the next thing they stung. But by God, if they weren't the prettiest nest of vipers he'd ever seen. In addition to Ruth, there were the two girls who looked enough alike that he was sure they were twins, from their dark, wavy hair to their hard-staring, big-lashed eyes to their proud chests and round hips. They also appeared to be sporting smears of axle grease on their hands and cheeks. And in their hands they each held a Winchester rifle.

The youngest was a fine-looking girl on her way to being a handsome woman—apparently one who could shoot, for she wore a double-gun rig in holsters on her hips. Just now her hands rested lightly on the butts, and on her perky little face sat narrowed eyes and a scowl, all directed his way. In the middle of them stood the short, stout woman who he could tell had been a great beauty herself before time and years of hard work tending a family had worn her down. He also guessed she was the matriarch of this deadly, pretty brood.

"Mama, this here is . . ." Ruth looked at Slocum. "I don't recall your name."

"That's because I never offered it. Nor you yours." He tucked the rifle under his arm and doffed his hat. "Ma'am. I'm John Slocum. Just passing through when this young lady got the drop on me. I'm afraid my horse bolted." He settled his hat back on his head. "Now if you'll excuse me, I'll just take my horse from out back there and be on my way. I was explaining to Ruth here that I am tracking a man and don't want to lose any more time."

He sidestepped toward the corner of the house, wanting nothing more than to get on the Appaloosa and ride on out of there. Quick as lightning, the twins cranked their rifles, the girl drew her side arms and cocked them, and the old woman ratcheted back the hammers on her double-barrel shotgun. "Course she did."

Slocum sighed, leaned the rifle against the house, and slowly slid his Colt into his holster. "Pardon me, ma'am?"

"I said course she got the drop on you. You're a man." The last word was pronounced much as Ruth had said it back on the ledge.

"There's no denying it," he said, careful to keep his hands raised. "Is that why you're so hostile toward me? A stranger? I have no truck with you. All I need is to move on and I aim to do that right now." He'd had enough of this fresh batch of fools. He turned to head down the side of the little house when a shot spanged the dirt inches in front of his left boot. He stopped. One of the twins, looking a bit pleased with herself, glared at him, a smirk breaking out at the edges of her perfect lips.

The old woman cackled. "You lucky that was Mary. 'Cause Angel don't miss."

Slocum glanced over at her and the old lady was bent double, yucking it up as if she'd told a real thigh slapper. And she seemed not to pay any heed to the cocked shotgun she waved near her offspring.

He stood less than two strides from the chipped corner of the little adobe house. All he had to do was dive, tuck into a roll, and he'd make it out of their way long enough to draw his Colt Navy. But what if he didn't? What if each one of these she-devils was equal to Mary's shot? Or better, as the old lady had hinted at?

"We're traveling women," said Ruth, still standing halfway between him and the others on the porch. When the rifle had been fired, the children had all clustered together at the far side of the house.

Slocum nodded. "Uh-huh, okay. So, where are you all traveling to?"

Ruth started to speak, but the old lady cut her off. "My daughter has a big mouth sometimes. Where we all are headed is none of your business."

"Why are you here, then? Planning on staying for long?"

The old lady sighed. "Again, stranger, I just don't see where that's any of your business."

"You got me there, ma'am. I'm just the curious type."

"Our wagon's busted."

"Ruth! You shut that blamed mouth, daughter!" The old lady shook a hard fist at the woman near Slocum.

Could be an in, he thought. A way to calm these women down enough for him to make his departure. "I have fixed wagons a time or two in the past. I'd be happy to take a look at it. No promises."

"We don't need no charity from strangers, and we darn sure don't need no help from a man. You hear me, Mr. Slocum?"

From the corner of his eye he saw Ruth fidgeting. Then she bolted toward him. He slicked out his Colt from his holster, expecting her to try some harebrained ambush. But she stood close to him, facing him, her hands loosely around his waist. She was protecting him from one of her trigger-happy siblings or from her mother.

Ruth glanced up at him briefly, then shouted over her shoulder. "We do need help, Mama. We been working on that axle for a day now and we need to get heading on!" To him, she said, "Walk with me toward the corner of the house."

They moved together. "Kind of like we're dancing," she said, her soft breath in his face, her breasts pushed against him more forcefully than was necessary, not that he minded. Before he could stop her, she snaked a hand over and grabbed her rifle from where he had leaned it.

He tensed, brought the Colt up, ready to drop her if she tried to position the rifle to shoot him. Instead she smiled at him and held the rifle out, away from them, but definitely gripped tight. She wasn't about to lose it to him a second time.

"Get on back there," she said, a smile flicking on her mouth.

"This is all well and good, Ruth, but how do I trust you or them? You're all bristling with weapons." He looked over her shoulder at the corner of the house they'd just slipped around, and the posse of kids were staring at them. "And children."

Ruth narrowed her eyes at them, but smiled. "You young'uns, get over here and help me show Mr. Slocum that wagon."

The other women clumped on through the ruin of the house and appeared out back, in much the same configuration as before. He didn't holster his Colt and neither did they ease off on the hammers of their respective weapons.

"Looks like we'll have to take you up on your kind offer . . . *sir.*"

"No need to call me that . . . *ma'am.* John or Slocum or both or neither is fine with me." Still he stood watching them.

"Oh, land's sake, Mama, put down them guns. Mary, Angel, you, too, and Judith? Holster them pistols before you shoot off your feet."

When they'd all eased off their respective weapons, Slocum looked around the rear of the place. There was a grassed paddock behind the house, and inside the paddock, four horses grazed, two riding horses and two bulkier workhorses, for pulling and, he suspected, farm chores. No wonder Tinker was so irate. They took not only themselves from his life, but also some of the tools he needed to make a go of farming.

It took Slocum a few moments to figure out just what had happened to the wagon. It was a damaged hub that had ended up breaking a number of spokes as the wheel wobbled its way off. They were lucky enough to break down near this place, and to be able to snub their two workhorses tight to the wagon and get it wheeled around back. But their spare wheel, another thing Slocum was relieved to see they had on hand, was not impressive. It was roughly the same diameter as the others, but the hub needed work.

It wasn't a cracked axle, for which he was grateful, because they weren't very well equipped with tools. But he'd still need to do a whole lot of carving and shaping to the hub. This shot all to hell his plans for catching up with Tunk Mueller. But he knew he'd never forgive himself if he left these women fending for themselves. Though he had to admit that they seem to be more than capable of taking matters into their own hands.

A half hour later, after wrestling with the thing, he had axle grease smeared on his hands and he knew that any second he was going to slip and the foul gunk would get all over his shirt, vest, and denims.

"Ruth?" he said as he peeled off his shirt. "I don't want to sound like I'm prying for information here, but—"

"Then don't." The old woman stood by the back steps to the little house, a ladle in one hand and sweat glistening on her brow. "And keep your clothes on."

Close by her mother stood the sullen young girl with the six-shooters. She kept her eye on Slocum and a sneer on her lips.

He lowered his voice and said, "Your mother and sisters don't seem any too pleased to have me helping out. I'm more than happy to ride on out of here."

She smiled at him, her own hands covered in grease. "I think you're full of it, and I also think that the twins are in a huff because you took their job. They wanted to fix this themselves. That's what they were working on before you showed up."

He nodded. That would explain the banging and ringing sounds. "Well, why don't they get over here and help?" He stood, eyeing the scant selection of tools they'd brought with them.

"Likely as not, because Mama told 'em to stay in the house."

"Sure, because I'm a man, and as we know, all men are evil."

Her smiled disappeared. "Most are," she said, not looking at him. "Least the ones I've known."

He was pretty sure that pursuing that line of thought would only make her angry again, and he'd had enough bickering with these women. He wanted to get the wagon fixed and get the heck out of there.

"You'll want a proper wheelwright to take a look at it once you get to the next decent-sized town."

Ruth nodded, holding the wheel in place while he scored the wood for another round of crude carving with his sheath knife. Not much longer and he'd have it.

"California. We're headed to California and want to make it over the Sierras before the snow flies."

"Oh, you don't have all that far to go, then. And it's still high summer, so you should be fine. Provided you get this wheel looked after." He looked at her, half smiling.

"Yes, sir," said Ruth, saluting him.

"That a truce of some sort?"

She shrugged. "Could be."

"Well, thank God for that."

Her playful smile disappeared once again and she said, "God?" she snorted. "I don't intend to thank Him for a thing. What's He ever done for any of us except heap misery down on our heads by the bucketful?"

"Amen, daughter," said the old woman, stepping down off the porch. The two women exchanged a look and then both started laughing. Slocum wiped his face with his balled-up shirt. The old lady's face seemed to lose ten years of hard living. The smile livened her entire appearance and Slocum could see clearly the beautiful woman that had raised such pretty daughters.

She looked at him, and kept the smile in place. "We are obliged to you for your assistance with the wagon. If you get your clothes back on, we'll be eating shortly. It ain't much, but it's what we got."

The meal was far more than he'd expected, considering the women looked to be traveling light. They'd unloaded their possessions into the broken-down house, and from what little he saw stacked inside, it seemed as if they had packed in a hurry and expected to move fast.

The family gathered around an old table in the center of the main room; crude benches had been set up along both sides. A crate at one end of the table served as his seat. "So," said Slocum, helping himself to a biscuit after the rest of them dove into the pile. "I take it you all don't say grace beforehand."

"Not anymore!" said a freckled little girl, smiling at him.

"Hush, child!" Ruth scowled at the girl and ladled steaming stew onto Slocum's pie-tin plate.

"We'll be buying supplies," said the old woman. "Restock the larder for the journey at Dalton's Corners. It's a few days west up the road from here. Know of it, Mr. Slocum?"

"I do, in fact, though I've only ever come into it from the west and left it headed southward. This road is new to me."

"Yep," said the old lady. "Not many folks travel this road. It's been a lonely valley for far too long for us—" She clapped her mouth shut and glanced quickly at him.

He said nothing, pretended that what she'd said didn't mean anything to him. In truth, it added to his guess that these were the women that the raging, sunburned, Bible-thumping farmer and his sons had lost. Besides, he'd seen no signs of bandits, so his suspicions had been confirmed much earlier.

With an image of the sunburned five in mind, he didn't blame these women one bit for leaving. But they must have been the ones to tie up the men. He shuddered involuntarily. These were dangerous, vengeful women. Women who appeared to be in a hurry. Question was—what finally made them leave?

He looked around the table at all the freshly scrubbed faces, young and older, and decided to hold his tongue for the time being. They obviously wanted to keep to their own business, and he had to remind himself that he had business of his own, too. "After this fine meal, I'll have to ride on out. That rascal won't catch himself. But I thank you kindly for your eventual hospitality." He smiled and was pleased to see the old woman did the same. "Now, I know how you reacted before, but I'm going to ask again anyway."

They all stopped eating and looked at him with sudden suspicion.

"You're sure you saw no other person. Hard fellow to miss. He might have been wearing a red shirt, sandy hair, needs a trim and a shave, shorter than me, and riding a dun mare?"

"We ain't seen him, that's a fact. But what did he do?" said the old woman, picking at her food.

He glanced at the children, then back to her. "Quite a few bad things. Bad as it gets. Killed innocent people. They were friends of mine."

The older lady's face grew stony, her eyes sad. "I am right sorry to hear that about your friends. I didn't mean to pry."

Ruth looked at him with questioning eyes. "You're following him to avenge your friends? Not for a reward?"

"No, I don't want any reward. I want him." He paused and again looked at the kids. "I want him to be punished for what he did. And so do a lot of other people."

"You can't leave, Mr. Slocum." Ruth gripped his forearm.

Her mother said, "And why not? The man has things to do and so do we. Like lighting a shuck for . . . other places. We need to be headed on out ourselves."

"I'd recommend you wait until first light, ma'am." Slocum looked out the open door at the waning light.

"Oh, I see," she said, setting down her spoon. "What's sauce for the goose ain't necessarily sauce for the gander, eh, Mr. Slocum?"

"That's exactly what I mean. But only because I have experience traveling at night and you don't. Besides, you'll be rested and ready to roll first thing in the morning."

"Well then, Mr. Slocum," said Ruth, showing him those glinting peepers again. "Why don't you take your own advice."

And the last thing he needed was for one of the kids to yawn. Soon, every mouth around the table, full of food or no, opened wide in a yawn, his included, try as he might to stifle it. He squinted at Ruth. "You planned that," he said, sighing and shaking his head. "I'll bunk down in the barn out back, head out at first light." He pushed back from the table and nodded toward the entire crew. "My compliments, ladies. That was one fine feed. Now, if you all will excuse me."

He'd been more tired than he'd expected. Within seconds he shucked his boots and once again unbuttoned his shirt and slipped out of it. He laid his head on his saddle and welcomed an easy sleep, his long, lean form stretched out on his bedroll on the dusty old hay in a back corner of the barn. He'd slept in more comfortable spots, but rarely one with so many curious creatures so close by. He drifted off to sleep, thinking thoughts of what might have been, particularly with that curious fire-brand named Ruth.

It was the faintest of scuffing sounds some hours later that snapped his eyes open. Even before he grew fully awake, rec-ognition became action and he slid his Colt Navy free from the holster where it lay in his coiled gun belt, close by his side. There it was again, a rustling, dragging sound. A snooping coyote? Doubtful. Rattler? Possible, then he thought for certain he heard someone swallow, a breath, faint but possible . . .

He cranked the hammer back. "Who's there?" he hissed, keeping low so spillover from the moonlight angling in through the open double doors—the doors themselves were long gone—didn't give him away.

"Mr. Slocum?" came the whispered reply. "Don't shoot."

"Ruth?"

She stepped into the light, and it shone through a light cot-ton nightgown, outlining her full form, and leaving little unimagined. She walked toward him. "Where are you?"

He sighed, eased the hammer back down, and holstered the Colt. "What do you think you're up to? Slinking around in the dark is a surefire way of getting shot."

"Oh, you wouldn't shoot me, Mr. Slocum."

"Don't be so sure. I may have killed for less than waking me up—you never know." He lay back down, his hands behind his head. "I was having such a nice dream, too."

He heard a quick fluttering sound, then felt her presence close by, even though he couldn't see much since she'd stepped away from the door and toward him into the darkened barn.

"As nice as this?" she whispered, closer than ever. He felt her breasts brush his bare arm and chest, her long hair against his face, her breath reminding him of mint somehow. Their lips brushed awkwardly, found each other, then he felt her tongue tip dart into his mouth, circle his lips. He felt himself thicken, his denims suddenly tight. Her fingers worked down there, alter-nately kneading and groping for the buttons, as he reached up and ran his callused hands along the smooth plane of her shoul-ders and back.

Slight sighing sounds escaped from her busy mouth. She managed to undo his buttons and helped him pull the jeans down. He freed one leg, though he wanted to work them off fully, but Ruth was having none of it. She climbed aboard him and trailed her busy mouth quickly down his chest, his belly, and wasted no time in engulfing his stiffest part in her warm, seeking mouth.

Up and down she worked him in a stunning rhythm, her teeth just scraping enough to tantalize him further. She let him go and licked him up and down as though it were a peppermint stick, a purring sound growing in her throat. His hands were tangled in her hair and his breath rasped. All too soon he had to ease her from her task.

"Whoa, girl. I might end up shooting you accidentally."

"Can't have that, Mr. Slocum."

Before he could answer, she worked her way back up and that magic tongue darted in between his teeth again as she lowered herself onto him, impaling with a sigh. As she sank down the length of his shaft, she trembled atop him, gripping his bottom lip lightly between her own and pausing there for just a moment.

He reached down the length of her again and massaged the velvety smooth swells of her backside. Then, as if by agreement, they each began to move in opposing but wholly comfortable directions, faster and faster. Soon, she sat up, arching her back and kneading his chest with her palms.

Her breath came in short gasps and then their motions grew tighter, shorter until together they paused, her fingers digging into his torso, his hands holding her tight to him. Then, with a gasp, she shoved herself up, then straight down on him. She gripped him hard down there, everything about her tense and trembling, before collapsing onto his chest, breathing hard but silently.

They stayed that way for some minutes, neither wanting to move. The night was cool but he felt her body covered in a sheen of light sweat. She raised her head, kissed him once, and with a sigh, she slipped up and off him.

"I'll be leaving early, Ruth."

"I know," she said as she slipped the nightgown over her head. "Good night, Mr. Slocum."

"Ruth, my name's John."

"I know . . . Mr. Slocum." And then, with a faint scuffing sound, she was gone.

For the second time that night, John Slocum lay back against his saddle and fell asleep, though this time he was smiling.

10

As it always did, something about the predawn hour awakened Slocum. He lay still in the brisk, creeping cool. Shapes emerged—stall posts, a broken plow, the crushed bottom half of an old steamer trunk—around the edges of the little ramshackle barn.

A sudden urge to leave, to put as many miles between himself and the traveling band of women, gripped him. He didn't want to give any more thought than he already had to that bewitching Ruth. He only still half believed that she'd come to him in the night like that. No sir, he told himself, there will be no more dallying with her, nor even thinking about her. Because, John Slocum, he told himself, that will only lead to bad things for a wandering man—all those kids and a trip to California. Unless the old woman shot him on sight for messing with her daughter. He smiled at the thought.

But he knew the women were the least of it. He felt a tremendous urgency to get back on Tunk's trail. He'd already lost a day and he didn't want to lose any more time. As it was, making up that time would be brutal, and Mueller was no slouch on the trail, from what Slocum knew of the foul man. He knew he'd done something heinous enough to warrant a tracker or several. Slocum still hoped he'd gotten an early enough jump on the man. He wanted him back in Arizona, any way he could.

He rolled from his blankets and within minutes, because he'd kept the Appaloosa poled apart from the women's four horses, he had the horse saddled. He cinched down his bedroll tight behind the cantle, double-knotting the thongs.

As he rode on out, he swore he heard a slight sound behind him. He looked back toward the silent little house in the gray light of early morning, but saw nothing moving, heard nothing else. Must have been one of the other horses. He kicked off toward the cleft in the canyon behind the house, straight north. No more travel on that westerly road.

He'd had good information that Tunk was bound to head north at some point, and since the women hadn't seen him, and he wagered that their word was truthful in this regard, might as well try to cut his trail sooner than later. This would also be a decent spot to climb out of the valley's north ridge he'd been paralleling for the past few days. Maybe he'd see something from up there. North it was.

He breathed deep of the fresh morning air. It felt good to be back out on the trail. The women were an interesting diversion, and he wished them well, certainly, but he admitted relief at being free of them and their problems. He hoped they got to wherever it was they were headed, knowing full well they were better off to get anywhere away from the crazy Bible-thumping old man, Tinker, than to stay with him. And it was a sure bet Tinker had no way of getting to them. He'd just as likely sit at his farm and wave his Bible around and scream about the she-devils who'd robbed him of a future.

Slocum knew that many people found great comfort in the Holy Bible, in following its teachings, but it wasn't something he'd felt particularly drawn to. He regarded it as something he might need one day, when he was old and feeble, if he made it that long, and to that end, he figured it was providing him comfort enough in that respect. But he was in no rush to figure out the rest.

As he rode on, he realized he didn't feel the need for any more religion in his day than what he saw waking up all around him. Soon, he sipped from his canteen. He'd gladly forgo coffee in favor of making up time. The horse was well rested and had fed on lush summer grass, and he had a canteen full of water, provisions enough in his saddle bags for a few more days. He breathed deep and admired the eddy and swirl of the low-lying fog as they passed through it, man and horse, alone in open country.

11

"We have made good time in gaining on the demons." Rufus Tinker nodded at the ground before them as if that were sufficient to explain his reasoning to his weary sons. They all could see the tracks in places as plain as day, though they meant little to them. No one had ever taught them to track anything more than a deer, and even when they had to do that, they followed animals they had plainly seen, then had shot and followed the blood trail. But rarely did they have to rely on reading sign.

Peter spoke up. "Papa, we have walked through the night and could all use a rest. We could fill our canteens at that stream, maybe nap for a spell. We are all tuckered out." He gestured at the other three men walking behind him. The brothers looked at the old man, then looked away, slight nods showing their agreement.

Tinker halted the mule and glared at each of his sons in turn. That they were exhausted was obvious, but he also didn't want to lose even more time. If they each had a mount, they could have all been on horseback, riding day and night. For that's what beasts of burden were for.

"Very well," he said, sliding from the mule. The old animal moaned in relief and lowered his head, fatigued. "We will stop for one hour. I will keep an eye on my timepiece. Get busy doing whatever it is you feel is so important that we must pause in this journey being undertaken in the name of God. I, for one, will not rest until those she-devils are safely trussed and accepting of the lash of the Lord's will, time and time again." He rubbed his bony red hands together.

Tinker felt himself warming to his topic, but stopped in mid-sentence as he turned his stony stare at each of his sons. They all seated themselves at the spot in the road where they'd stopped, their weapons and packs still in their arms and slung on their backs.

"Lazy loafing idlers. The Lord will require punishment when we return to the farm. The Lord will not be cheated out of His tribute."

Light snores were the only response.

"Pah!" said the old man. He pulled out his pocket watch and tapped the face. It hadn't worked in years, but he referred to it throughout each day because he knew it made him appear commanding, and he knew that he was nothing if not their leader. He was more than their father. He was their spiritual guide, their master, the very Right Hand on Earth of the Lord! He trembled with the thought of it. These fools and the women, nothing more than lazy, fleshy conveyances sent to test him. He would not fail.

Rufus Tinker tied the mule to a branch, sat back against a rock, and despite the fact that he had done nothing but ride all day, he soon fell asleep as well.

12

With each mile kicked off behind him, and with each new ray of sunlight from the east warming first his right side, then his entire body, Slocum felt renewed. Fleeting images of the sun-burned men, the beauty of the women who had left them behind, all mingled in his mind and he decided not to force them away any longer. They were, after all, more experiences that helped make up this far-ranging life he was leading.

By the time he crested the northern edge of the valley, the sun was a full-burning thing threatening to become its old demon self. Well, let it burn. He had a full head of steam and Mueller was somewhere up ahead. He hoped. They paused at the top, and he edged the horse in among a stand of aspen, taking care that he'd not be skylined should someone look up his way, and he fished his brass telescoping spyglass from his saddle bag. He'd bought it off an old Basque sheepherder not long before, and though he'd owned other such devices in the past, this one was of exceptional quality. He vowed to try to hang on to it. At least until he got bushwhacked and robbed again. The thought of the last time that had happened still rankled him.

Within a minute of scanning the immediate countryside below him, then edging outward with each slow pass of the glass, he was rewarded with sign of what could well prove to be smoke from a campfire. A thin gray haze drizzled upward from a dense patch of trees to the northwest a good three miles below.

Can't be Mueller, he thought. Why wouldn't he be farther ahead? Just because he hadn't been here before didn't mean lots of other folks didn't travel through the region, or better yet, call it home. No, I am probably looking at someone's stove smoke.

But he couldn't afford to ignore it. As he collapsed the brass tube down into itself and reached to stuff it into his saddlebag, he heard a slight sound, and paused. Not moving his head, but scanning the gradual slope behind him. Was someone tailing him? His eyes roved, then he saw it, a jerking, flitting brown-and-black thing—a ground squirrel poked its nose in the air. He smiled at it and at himself for thinking it was tracking him, and made secure the flap on the saddlebag.

"Come on, horse. Enough foolishness." They picked their way down the northern slope of the ridge, doing their best to keep to the shadows and trees for as long as he was able.

The farther downslope he traveled, the more convinced Slocum became that he wouldn't find too many settlers on this side of the ridge. As hospitable and green and promising as the valley to the south had been, this was arid land with only the high-summer promise of growth to offer. But he knew that never lasted long. These lush months soon passed and gave way to cold, blowing snows. And when it did rain, it came in short, harsh bursts that more often than not ran off the caked earth instead of staying and nourishing. So whose smoke had he spied? And was it smoke at all?

The landscape that spread before him was hilled and pocked with tangles of wind-twisted thickets, stands of mixed-growth trees, and knobs of jagged rock upthrust from already-browned hummocks of sparse grasses gone wispy in the heat and wind.

He managed to make his way down in relative concealment, and once in the trees, though he was still a long way from where he'd spied the smoke, the horse's ears pricked forward and Slocum reined up and followed suit, canting his head to the side in an effort to better hear . . . nothing. But the horse's muzzle quivered, its nostrils working the air. Slocum's, too. And he was rewarded with the faint but unmistakable tang of wood smoke, carried to him, thankfully, on a light southward breeze.

He doubted it was Tunk Mueller, but whoever it was might have had dealings with the outlaw, or at least seen him. And hopefully he'd left them unhurt and alive. He urged the Appaloosa forward at a faster walk. They were hidden by a slight rise—he'd take his advantages where he could get them. As he emerged from behind it, he saw a red blur moving behind trees. It looked like a shirt, someone who appeared to be moving in no hurry— puttering about a campsite maybe. He had to get up close without being seen, the red shirt all but convincing him that it was indeed a slow-traveling Mueller. But he had to be sure.

He ground-tied the Appaloosa well away from his quarry, near a patch of stringy, somewhat green grass. The horse didn't seem to mind. He set to it with a fervor Slocum himself usually reserved for large meals. Take it where you can, I guess. He shucked his rifle from its sheath and cat-footed around the gray, tumble-down boulders separating him from this mysterious red-shirted person.

He'd made it to within a few dozen yards, nearly to the curious campsite, when from behind him, a rattle of collective sounds froze him in his low-crawling crouch. What the hell was that? A mix of the sounds of nickering horse and tumbling rocks . . . He ducked down behind the boulder he was skirting. He risked a peek around the side of the nearest boulder and just caught a glimpse of something straight back behind the Appaloosa, closer to the slope they'd traveled down.

Damn if it wasn't a person. Someone in a light shirt and a skirt? No . . . and then an image of Ruth flashed in his mind. She'd been wearing pants, but . . . Oh no, it couldn't be that foolish woman! He jerked his head back toward Red Shirt and saw nothing. Great.

Caught, Slocum. You're caught betwixt a mess of rocks, a potential killer, and a cow-eyed woman. He risked another peek around the boulder and a rifle shot whanged off one far behind, near his horse. The woman let out a strangled yelp.

So Red Shirt was either Mueller or an innocent. But whoever it was, he wasn't afraid to fling lead. As if to put a wax stamp on the thought, another round did much the same as the first, and elicited the same response from the woman. Slocum's horse nickered louder and galloped off. Fortunately, Slocum knew that the beast wouldn't go far. There was plenty of graze and the horse was always hungry.

It was possible that Red Shirt didn't know he was here, trapped between him and the woman. Slocum didn't see any other horses, so whoever it was must have either walked, which was unlikely, or left her own horse back up at the top of the hill. Maybe he could belly-crawl off to the right, snake his way around in a wide arc. But that wouldn't help Ruth, if that's who it was, though he was relatively sure it was her, darn her silky hide.

A dozen feet to his right sat a cairn, the stones left by some act of nature long before man ever thought to set foot here. From there on out, it would be a smoother crawl of it, with plenty of cover for him to dash to, between where he was and Red Shirt's campsite. He wasn't risking any intrusion, which told Slocum that the mystery man was up to no good and so, probably, was Mueller. One way to find out, Slocum old boy, he told himself, and slunk forward.

The next shot rang out, spanging off a nearby boulder, sending stinging rock chips skyward, and letting Slocum know the man must know he was there. But did he know who Slocum was? He wanted nothing more than to get a clear shot at the bastard, put him down once and for all. But between the distance, the fact that he was well hidden, and the slim chance that he might not be Mueller, Slocum couldn't risk a killing shot. He had to know. He had to get closer.

He was busy dashing from the tumbledown of boulders to the horse-size cairn when, from behind him, the woman, no doubt scurrying for better cover, knocked loose a fresh tumble of rocks. Red Shirt let go another two-shot volley, then must have seen Slocum, because the next thing he knew, even as he dove for the cover of the cairn ahead, a bullet blazed a smoking, seeping red trench across his thigh. He pitched sideways and his teeth came together hard. He growled as he pushed himself forward to get to cover. Going backward—which would provide better cover—would take too long. God, but that hurt.

He'd been grazed plenty, but this was a deeper wound. And all because of that damned woman. If he ever had the chance to get his hands on her again, he'd not be so kind. Even as it welled red with fresh blood, Slocum was grateful it hadn't been an inch lower, or he might have to dig out a lead pill from his leg—if he could. Two inches lower and he'd have had to deal with a shattered bone. Mueller, or whoever Red Shirt was, was a decent shot.

For long minutes afterward, all was still. The sun soaked into everything, driving even the buzzing heat-loving insects to silence. Slocum finished wrapping his kerchief tight around his leg to help slow the bleeding, and wished he had his saddle-bags at hand, and especially that flask-size bottle of bourbon he kept secreted in there, mostly for mornings when the camp-fire was slow to catch and the temperatures were still too nippy.

He wormed himself into a more comfortable position, then lay low, hat pulled down, leg throbbing like a locomotive churning at the station just before a journey. Waiting out your enemy was the only tactic he'd ever found effective against gun scum. He only hoped he had enough wherewithal to wait out old Red Shirt. This was one wily and patient man.

At least I don't have to worry if the woman has gotten herself shot, he thought. I'd surely have heard that racket.

Time passed slowly. Slocum would occasionally hear a horse-shoe strike stone, and knew the Appaloosa was well, if fidgety. He heard nothing of the woman and had grown increasingly worried. Maybe she had taken a shot after all. From all meager indications, Red Shirt was a decent shot. He figured the better part of a half hour had passed and he knew he couldn't sit there and bleed to death. He had to do something. He bent low and craned his head, close to the ground, around the far right side of the bottom-most boulder he'd been hiding behind. No sign of that red garment.

He pulled his head back, turtle-like, and another shot spanged off the rock close by, sending a spray of slicing chips at him. He covered his face with his forearms, but the rock fragments cut his arms and showered all around him. Enough was enough. Even if it was Tunk and even if he did know Slocum was tailing him, which he'd thought was all but impossible, Slocum had to end this thing.

"Hey!" he shouted in a voice lower than his normal tone. Just in case he was still clueless, it wouldn't do to have Mueller recognize him. "You there, in the red shirt!"

The paused was long enough that Slocum thought for sure the man wasn't interested in a parley. Then the man's voice barked, "Whatta you want?"

Could well be Mueller. Sounded a bit like him, but it was raspy and frenzied, hard to tell. "I want to know why you're shooting," said Slocum. "I'm just passing through—no call to shoot at me."

"I didn't shoot at you, I shot you. I seen it. And you ain't alone."

Slocum shifted, hoping to catch sight of the man. He grimaced as fresh arrows of pain lanced up his leg. He had to get up soon or he'd be too stiff to do much of anything except lie here and get blood poisoning. "You sound distrustful," he shouted back. "Like you're a wanted man."

Another long minute passed and Slocum was about to raise the stakes and start firing, anything to distract the man and give himself a chance to stand up, when he saw a quick burst of smoke rise up where before there had only been light smoke wafting from the man's campfire—but this was the fast rising, billowing sort of smoke you get from a doused fire. Something was about to happen. And it did—within seconds, Slocum heard hoofbeats receding. He risked another glance around the rock. Sure enough, through the trees he saw a red shirt moving away fast, on horseback. On one of the Monktons' mounts, he bet, damn him. Slocum felt sure that it had been Tunk Mueller, though why the man had chosen to stop here was beyond him. He should have been well past this point by now. Unless he truly hadn't expected to be tailed.

Great, thought Slocum, now he'll be tipped off and will move faster and with more caution than before. And I'm slowed up with a grazed, bleeding leg.

Using his rifle and the rock, he managed to get his feet under him. A wash of hot pain rose up from the afflicted limb and over him as if he were dunked in a lake of fire. It abated enough for him to lift the rifle, train it in the direction the shooter had been. He was pretty sure Mueller had been alone, but it didn't pay to take chances. He also wanted that annoying woman to see him—he was sure she'd scramble down to him.

He didn't have long to wait. Her footsteps were loud, not cautious, setting still more rocks to tumble. He kept a narrowed gaze at the copse of trees ahead, waited for her to come to him.

Finally, she was close enough to talk with, and he turned, ready for a fight. "What in the hell was that all ab—"

It wasn't Ruth at all. It was her younger sister, Judith, the one who'd scowled at him the entire time he'd been with the family. And she was still wearing her six-shooters.

As he looked at her, he recalled the few times earlier that day on the trail when he thought he'd heard something behind him. It hadn't been the horses or the squirrel. It hadn't been anything other than the damned girl. He was torn between anger and amazement. "What are you doing here?"

Judith saw his gashed, bleeding leg. "You've been shot!"

"Yeah, no thanks to you. And I lost Mueller."

"You blame me?" She resumed her customary scowl.

"You bet I blame you, little miss."

"How dare you say that. I been keeping an eye on you."

"It's been long years since I needed a wet nurse, by God. Besides, you're a child. I doubt you can even handle those things." He nodded toward her six-guns.

She tried to meet his gaze, tried to muster up her old scowl, but just couldn't do it. She looked at the ground, her hands resting on the butts of her pistols.

"Well, hell," said Slocum. He sighed and watched as the red-shirted man finally disappeared in the distance. "Are you hurt at all?"

She shook her head. Scolded like that, she looked more like a child than a young woman.

"Good. Might as well make yourself useful and fetch my horse."

"But you need to doctor that wound . . ."

"That's why I asked you to get my horse. I have supplies in my saddlebags."

"Oh." She nodded and headed toward the Appaloosa, who'd wandered away when the shooting began.

While he waited, Slocum turned around and leaned against the boulder, the effort causing a wave of black dizziness to overcome him. He gritted his teeth, not wanting to pass out. This day, heck, this entire week was not going at all as he had expected it would. When the wave eased up, he risked a look at the wound. It was, as he suspected, worse than he'd initially thought. Deeper and bleeding more. He'd heal, but he really should sew it up. He'd sewn his own wounds before, but this one was long, as long as his hand. That bullet had plowed a furrow as deep and as wide as a finger, carrying a whole lot of meat with it.

She returned with the horse, secured the reins to a tree limb, and eyed him. "You don't look so good."

"Course not," he managed to say. "I've been shot."

She kept silent, untied the bags, and slid them off the horse. They were heavy for her, but she gamely hefted them onto her shoulder and lugged them to him.

"Thanks," he said, unbuckling the bags. As he rummaged, he asked about her own mount.

"I left it up yonder, at the top of the hill."

"Won't your family miss it? And speaking of such things, won't they miss you?"

"I am growed enough to make my own choices."

"And what choice would that be?" He peeled apart the edges of his denims that had matted into the wound. "Ahh," he said through gritted teeth, trying to keep from shouting. The blood had begun to dry, but freeing the tattered edges of fabric set it flowing again. "Dammit," he muttered, sweat stippling his forehead. He felt cold and that dizzy feeling threatened to overtake him again. "Help, please . . ."

But she had already begun to take over, gently pushing his own hands away from the wound. "First thing, we need to get the weight off it. Move over to your left and sit on that lower rock so I can fix you up proper."

He did as she asked and said, "You're going to have to sew it up."

That didn't seem to bother her. She just nodded. "Got to clean it first."

"Whiskey." He motioned with a finger. "In the bag."

She pulled out the glass flask and he took it, knocked back a couple of gurgles, then handed it to her. It helped clear his head. Good thing, too, as she didn't waste any time and poured it right on the wound.

"Damn, Sam!" Oddly, the pain and the booze both went to his head. Blood welled in the wound again, but it didn't look so bad that they couldn't sew it up. "I'll tell you how to do it, and help you, so we get it cinched up. At least it should slow the bleeding."

They built a small fire no bigger than what he could hold in his cupped palms to sterilize the needle, then poured whiskey on it and the wound. They worked at it together, though it took a slow, painful hour. Most of it consisted of Slocum helping her poke the dulled saddle needle through his ornery hide, then gritting his teeth and looking forward to a few swigs of whiskey once they were done. By the time they had finished, most of his spare shirt and her kerchief were soaked in blood.

When the grisly task was over, he took another swallow of whiskey. "It'll be a puckered scar, no doubt, but it could have been a whole lot worse."

"Now?" she said as she finished putting everything back in the bags and draping them behind the saddle's cantle.

"Now you help me into my saddle. I have to check that camp. See if he left behind any sign verifying who he was, where he might've been headed."

"But you can't ride. We . . . we should make a camp. Use his. You said yourself he's not coming back, right?"

"Wrong. Here's where we part ways."

She looked alarmed and crushed, all at once.

"Look, Judith. I have a job to do and you have a family to get back to."

She said nothing, but led his horse away from him, just out of his reach. He stiff-legged it over toward her, but she was too quick for him and jumped aboard the beast.

"You get back here right now, Judith!" He'd had enough of

her games but the girl just smiled at him and booted the horse toward Mueller's little camp.

"I'll look at it for you and be back right quick."

The commotion forced more blood through the stitching in his leg and he felt weaker by the minute. He watched her ride, knowing she was safe. They'd both seen Mueller headed north-ward. He was grateful Mueller still wore that red shirt, made him easy to spot at a distance. He doubted she'd find anything but a smoldering campfire. Hell, he thought, might as well do what she'd said and move on into Mueller's camp himself for the night.

In fact, he'd have to camp here, he knew that now. But he wouldn't tell her that. He'd send her back up the hill to her horse. It would be dark in another few hours, but he'd make sure she was long gone back to her kin at their run-down place. He knew they'd be sick with worry over her. They'd lost a whole day in worry over her, he bet. And they'd be anxious to be on their way toward California.

The word seemed to ring in his head, as though it had been shouted down a deep, dark well . . .

13

He must have been worse off than he knew, because the next time he looked up, she was just a few yards away, atop the Appaloosa, looking down at him.

"You don't look so good, Mr. Slocum. In fact, you look downright awful. No color at all, unless you call gray a color."

"I appreciate your concern and your help with my leg—"

She cut him off. "Don't you want to know what I found at the bandit's camp?"

He stared at her for a moment. The girl didn't seem to make sense. Then he remembered what she'd been doing. He cursed himself for not keeping his mind focused. "Yes, yes, okay. What did you find?"

"Nothing but a campfire it looked like he had urinated on."

Again, Slocum shook his head. He didn't believe he'd ever heard a woman say that word. This trip was not going at all like he'd planned. He had been sure up until two days ago that he would have found Tunk Mueller and have been halfway back to Arizona by now. He closed his eyes and sighed.

"Judith," he said, not opening his eyes. "I have a job to do and the life I live is no place for a woman, let alone a young one. You need to go on to California with your family, make a life for

71

yourself. You understand me?" He tried not to look at the silent teardrops rolling down her young cheeks, dripping off the end of her perfect little nose. She was just a confused kid.

"But I wanted to go with you. I meant to. I . . . I don't want to go with them. They . . . they beat me!"

He had to smile at the unlikely thought of it. "It's true I didn't spend much time with your mother and sister and the others, just a few hours, really, but they didn't seem the type to hit a child. At least not like that bill of goods you're trying to sell me."

"I can be useful to you. I got these guns. I can use 'em, too. Mama said that women should know how to shoot."

"What about your father? What did he say?"

Her jaw thrust outward. "What do you know about him?"

He shook his head and shrugged, not wanting to dredge up something she didn't want to discuss. Not yet anyway But the conversation seemed to revive him, and he felt better than he had minutes before.

She stepped down off the horse and he stood up.

"If you work at it, you could well become famous one day for using those. If it means as much to you as you say it does."

"What do you mean?" She dragged a hand across her eyes, trying hard to overcome her crying.

"Now I don't mean as an outlaw." He smiled again, tried to get her to do the same. It worked a bit. He struggled and, with her help, managed to saddle up.

"I mean you might become a trick-shot artist," he said, catching his breath. Climbing into the saddle had taken a mighty effort, and he felt shaky and had broken a sweat. "All the famous ones are women. Traveling shows and the like, and someone as pretty as you should be able to find her way into a theatrical troupe without too much worry. If you can shoot."

She looked up at him, narrowed her eyes, and they took on that hard look again. "You're funnin' me."

"No, ma'am. I would not do that. But I am moving on, and you're not coming with me. Is that understood?"

She scowled at the ground again, then looked at him through

hooded eyes. "Least you can do is ride me back up that hill to my horse. It's a long walk."

Slocum looked up the hill. She did help him with his leg. Even though she caused it. He sighed, kicked a foot out of the stirrup, and lowered an arm. "Let's go," he said, swinging her up behind him in the saddle. It was a tight fit and he suspected she was enjoying it more than he was. She might well one day be as pretty or prettier than her older sisters, but right now she was a child playing games and all he wanted to do was get her to her horse and point her toward her family. She'd be there within a few hours. The country was desolate enough that he doubted she'd get herself in any trouble.

As the Appaloosa, with a few booted urgings from Slocum, switch-backed up the slope, dark, worrisome thoughts came to Slocum with each step upward. What if she did run into trouble? Where there was one outlaw, there was bound to be another. Or what if her horse were to spook a rattler or shy up for any reason at all? She could get thrown, hit her head, and lie there dying, and no one would ever know.

Stop it, he told himself. You keep thinking like that, you'll lose out on your fast-retreating chance to catch up with Tunk Mueller. Dump her onto her horse and hightail it north while you still have strength and a chance. But as he reached the top, he knew that, despite everything his free-ranging spirit was shouting at him to do, he ought not leave the girl alone. He'd escort her back to her family, then head north, once again, onto Mueller's cooling trail. It would mean another day gone, but what could he do? She was just a kid.

They reached the top and he recognized the stand of trees through which he'd cut downward hours before. "Where'd you leave your horse, Judith?"

She didn't answer.

"Hey, Judith, where did you tie your mount?"

"I . . . I don't see it." There was genuine fear in her voice.

"What do you mean? You had to have a horse to follow me that close, so where is it? No games now, Judith."

She slipped down from behind him and the Appaloosa fidgeted.

"It was the mare. She was right here, I swear it." She rubbed a low branch on a yellow pine and looked at him. "But she's gone. Oh, Mama's going to tan me for certain."

"Yeah, and for more than one thing, I reckon." He kicked out of the stirrup and extended his arm again. "Come on, we'll track it. Like as not, it headed back the way you came, homeward bound for a bait of feed. We might just catch up with it. Then you'll at least be in trouble for one less thing."

"Are you going to tell . . . about me running away, I mean?"

"I don't think I'll have to, do you?"

As they rode, the afternoon's waning light and heat, and the insect buzz around them, lulled them into a silence that they maintained for a few miles. Then close to his ear, Judith said, "Mr. Slocum."

It startled him a bit, but he said, "Mm-hm?"

"I seen you. Last night, I mean. You and Ruth."

His guts tightened and he felt as if he'd been punched. He cleared his throat. "I don't know what you—"

"I am not a child, Mr. Slocum. I understand how these things work."

"Then you should also know there are certain things that are private affairs and nobody's business. You understand? That was none of yours. Your sister and I are both adults and—"

"You got no call to be angry. Just wondered what she was up to, is all. I figured I'd follow her. I couldn't really see all that well anyway. Not much at all, truth be told."

"Well, good. Because it's none of your business."

"I know, I know. You already said that."

Slocum reined up and turned in the saddle to see her face. "Look, Judith. You can't go around following people. It's just not right."

"Isn't that what you're doing with that Turkey fella?"

He had to admit her point, and smiled. "Tunk, yeah, well, it's not quite the same thing. He's a bad person. A killer, and I aim to bring him in to see that he pays for his crimes. The law will decide his fate. But you have given me an idea."

"What's that?"

"An idea how you can make a living someday. You are a

natural born snoop. You could be a lady detective. If you're genuinely handy with those peashooters of yours, it's a damn sight more useful to society than being a trick-shot artist."

"But I was warming to that notion. Being on the stage and all."

"Yeah, but detectives get to stop bad folks, and they get to wear disguises doing it."

"Really?"

"Sure," he said. "Don't you ever read the dime novels?"

"Oh no, Papa says they're the devil's work." She stopped talking as fast as she'd begun.

At the mention of her father, Slocum thought of the sunburned men. If the old man with the big beard, the wild eyes, and the preachy speechifying was her father, then that meant that Ruth and the twins were his daughters as well. And that meant that the other men were their brothers. Surely the old man didn't mean that these women were their own brothers' wives? If that were the case, did that mean they fathered their own nieces?

He'd heard about such nests of strange families tucked in the hills, especially back in Georgia, where he'd grown up. But such stories had always struck him as too strange to have much truth behind them. Besides, these women and the kids all seemed normal, not tetched. Well, not outwardly anyway.

They passed a few minutes in silence, then Judith said, "How's your leg?"

"I'll live—thanks and no thanks to you." He glanced at her to let her know he was only partly serious.

Before she could offer up what he was sure would be a biting response, they heard a shout from up ahead. A rider came toward them, rounding a cluster of boulders. Dark hair, no hat, and it looked to Slocum as if it was a woman. The rider was leading a second horse, riderless.

"I do believe that's Ruth." Slocum pulled his hat low over his forehead.

"Oh boy," said Judith. And as they rode closer, Slocum was inclined to agree with Judith's remark. Ruth's pretty face was set in a scowl of rage. Even from fifty feet out, she hurled a string of harsh oaths at them, some of which Slocum wasn't sure he'd ever heard before—and certainly not from a woman. They rode within ten feet of each other and Ruth kept right on barking and growling in anger that looked to be directed all at Slocum.

When she stopped long enough to draw a breath, he dove in with a quick volley of his own. "Good thing she was along, else I might not be here." He turned the horse enough that Ruth could see his bloodied pant leg and the puckered, raw wound sticking out of it, swollen and bristling with tag ends of thread. He'd not looked down at the wound in a while, but it had grown more swollen and looked god-awful.

The sight of it at least had the pleasant effect of shutting up Ruth's tirade. Even if only for a moment. Her face softened and she hopped down off her horse. She approached him with her hands out as if she were approaching a wounded bird.

When it looked as though she were about to touch it, he said, "Easy, I don't want a blasted thing to graze it. It's mighty tender just now. Truth is, I'm about spent and I expect Judith is, too. We had a big day. If I remember right, we're not far from your encampment."

That seemed to snap Ruth out of her daze of sympathy for him. "Yes, another twenty minutes or so should have us back there. I . . . I found Judith's horse." She looked at her sister with more relief than anger. "I've been looking most of the day. And when I found it, I feared the worst. I thought for sure you were laying bleeding to death somewhere."

Slocum cleared his throat. "If you don't mind, I'd like to partake of your hospitality once again. I could use a decent night's rest, ride out again first light."

"Like you did today, huh?"

"Yes, just like I said I would." He stared straight at her, not letting her try to imply anything that hadn't already been covered between them the night before.

Her face softened again. "Mount up, Judith. Mama's got a few choice words for you, I expect." She turned to Slocum. "And you, you look terrible . . . John."

He offered a weary smile. "I expect I do. I'm not usually at my best when I've been shot."

"Mama's good with injuries. She'll fix you up in no time."

All those kids and men, I expect she'd have to be, he thought. As they headed back to the little run-down house with all the kids and women, Slocum had to admit it would be better than spending the night alone out in the foothills, but he knew that was only the throbbing pain in his leg talking.

The terrain was familiar to him, and he knew when they were drawing close. He fancied he could almost smell a pot of bubbling stew. And then they heard gunfire. And not just a random shot, but a volley. Up the last rise and there before them was the little tumbledown place, the wagon still out back, the little barn off to the left of the corral, and no people in sight. But a whole lot of smoke rose into the air from gunshots from the ridge directly across the trail from the house, close by. Dangerously close.

Slocum booted his horse into a gallop, barely outdistancing the two sisters on their own mounts. "Who'd be shooting at your family?" he shouted, not really needing an answer, for even as he asked it, he knew. And the looks on their faces told him his suspicions were probably right.

14

From the location of the flashes peppering the hillside across from the little house, it looked to Slocum as if there were four or five guns raining lead down on the place. He hustled the two women and their mounts into the barn and found that someone had already put the two workhorses in as well. The structure would keep them relatively safe, unless it caught fire. And would also prevent whoever it was attacking from stealing or running off the horses.

He slid his rifle from its boot, and stuffed extra shells into his pockets. "We have to get to the house, see if your family's okay. You two go first, don't waste time. I'll cover you, then you do the same as I head to the wagon, halfway between the barn and house. Ready? I'll say 'Go!' and you make tracks, got me?"

The sisters nodded to him and crouched low, holding hands.

"Go! Go! Go!" Slocum ripped off one shot after another into the trees and rocks across the trail, then managed two more rounds as he hightailed it, stiff-legged and hobble-running, toward the house. Within seconds, he joined the rest in the little thick-walled adobe house. It would withstand a lot of bullets. He only hoped the attackers didn't have anything that they might toss at them through the sagged, hole-filled roof.

Slocum was relieved to note everyone seemed to be unhurt and clustered in the rearmost—and safest—corner of the house. Shots from their attackers echoed at random. Occasional shouts, unintelligible, reached his ears. They were the voices of men, but beyond that, he didn't know what was being shouted.

The littlest ones were visibly frightened, whimpering and huddled under blankets, but there was little that Slocum could do, at least during daylight. Even then, he wondered how useful he'd be to them now that his mobility was limited.

"Ma'am," he said to the old lady, who wasn't budging from her position just behind the shutter at the front window. "What's going on here?"

Without looking at him, she snorted, said, "What does it look like? We're being shot at."

He joined her at the window, peeked carefully outside, the fading afternoon light revealing even less than mere moments before. "How long's it been going on?" Before she could answer him, a shot spanged off the edge of the window inches from his face. "Damn!"

The old woman laughed.

"So who is it, do you know?"

She looked at him, but said nothing.

"Your husband and sons?"

That pulled her from her post by the window, and riveted every other eye in the place on him, too. "How'd you know?" Her voice was low, cold, and measured.

"How do you think? Before I arrived here yesterday, I came right by their place, found them lashed to fence posts out front, naked and nearly dead, sunburned beyond belief. I'd never seen anybody looking so bad off from the sun. It would have been funny, but a few more hours and they'd have surely been dead." He watched their faces, and saw horror and worry there.

"Nearly dead, you say?" The old woman looked at the rifle in her hands, then spoke in a low voice, almost to herself. "Thought for sure they would have slipped them ropes in short order." She looked up at him, a weird mixture of relief and anger on her face. "Only trying to buy us some time . . ."

"That would explain why they didn't follow along until

now," said one of the twins. "We were just trying to give ourselves extra time to skedaddle, is all . . ."

The mother looked at him. "We never expected to break
down so close to home."

"In that wagon?" said Slocum. "You'd be lucky to make it
another day or two without something else giving out."

He peered out another window hole. "He wasn't too happy
when I left them. Talking all sorts of religious stuff, God this
and God that and devil this and devil that and seasoning his
speechifying with big words I've never heard a preacher use."

The old lady snorted. "That's 'cause he ain't a preacher. He
ain't much of anything—bad father, lousy husband, even worse
farmer. 'Bout all he's good for is making babies." She glanced
at the huddled children and her daughters as she resumed her
post by the window. "Wonder how he got them guns."

"You know well as I do, Mama, that he had them hidden
away in that hidey-hole in the barn," said Ruth.

The old lady nodded. "Wish I had known how many he had
down there. We tried to break through them strap hinges, but
it was sealed up tight and we had to get while the getting was
upon us."

Another volley rang out and the little house received another
good peppering. "Dang them! Don't they know we got kids in
here?" The old lady shouted out the window, "Hey! I know it's
you, you old God-lovin' savage!"

In response, she received another fresh round. From the
other side of the front door, Ruth let out a sharp cry and spun
into the back of the room, knocking into the wooden table. She
clutched her shoulder.

Her mother and one of the twins went to her and soon had
her seated with the children. "Hush now, hush now, it was only
a grazing," said the old woman to quiet the crying children.
"She'll be right as rain in no time."

Slocum looked back toward Ruth, met her gaze. She seemed
clear-eyed. Pained, sure, but she didn't seem like one for faint-
ing. They exchanged nods. He turned back to the window, wondering about the mess he'd stumbled into. "What kind of people
would shoot their own family?"

"The kind that don't care about them. The kind who only wants breeding stock. That's what he called us. Breeding stock!" The old woman sneered as she bandaged Ruth's wound, and directed a look of pure, smoldering hate toward the window. Slocum felt sure the rascals hunkered down somewhere in those woods felt her anger.

"Is that what this is all about? You ran away because you weren't appreciated, is that it?"

"Isn't that enough?" said Ruth. "You make it sound as if we should have stayed and put up with it."

"No, I'm surprised you didn't leave sooner."

As full dark settled down about them outside, Slocum warned them against lighting the oil lamp. "They obviously don't care about you or the children, and have proven they'll shoot to harm, or worse, so I'd keep the light to a minimum, at least until I can figure out where they're holed up. Or if they're creeping up on us."

"You think they'd do that?"

"Yep. I would if I had my prey pinned down in a little house. I'd do my best to make sure no one could leave."

From outside, a sharp voice rang out. "Hey, in the house!"

"It's him," said the old woman to the people in the room. Then she shouted out the window, "What do you want, you beast?"

"You come back home now. You've made your point, but you all are just women! The Good Lord saw fit to give you to us, but His teachings tell us that second-class citizens ain't allowed to express themselves such as you have done here. Now come back home and one month's worth of lashes and fasting will be the only punishment, you have my word on that! But I warn you, any more of this foolishness and the Good Lord will guide my hands to exceed the reach of the lash! You have received but a taste of His mighty vengeance!"

"This is foolish. I'm going out there to stop this old thumper once and for all."

"This ain't your fight, Mr. Slocum. You leave him be, you leave them to us."

"Like hell I will. He's got me pinned down here, too. But

he's shooting at you. Hell, he already shot one of you." He gestured at Ruth. "He's turned his own sons against his own wife and daughters and grandchildren."

Slocum wasn't actually quite sure what the family arrangement was, but the members didn't seem to be all that afflicted with inbreeding. Maybe some of them were from outside. He didn't really care at that moment; he only wanted to put an end to it, by putting a bullet in the old man's head if need be.

Despite his brief bit of late-night fun with Ruth, this family, both sides, had caused him more harm than good. And all he wanted now was to get the heck out of there. But like it or not, he was smack-dab in the middle of their family feud.

"You all keep your heads down. I have something to do. I'll be back." He ignored the volley of voices that begged him to stay, not to go out in the dark. But he knew the cover of night could be a blade that cut both ways. He slipped out the back door, and stopped short when he heard the old matriarch behind him.

"Whatever you do, don't you kill my babies, Mr. Slocum. They might be devils, but they're still my sons."

"I understand, ma'am, but I can't promise they won't die if they draw on me."

He took advantage of the near dark and stiff-legged his way into the night. He kept low, made straight out back behind the place, then angled right and hobbled around the corral, then the barn. He was rewarded with the flare of a match a few hundred feet away. Someone else was taking advantage of the cover of darkness, and coming closer, from the sounds of it—and they were none too quiet, sounding as if it were a blind bear.

Judging from the size of the older boys, they were quite capable of resembling bears. Slocum cat-footed around the end of the barn and paused at the edge of the road. There were the footsteps again. Stopping, then starting, someone was also waiting to hear the footfalls of an opponent. Slocum wouldn't give him the courtesy, though. He waited him out. When he heard the other person's boots on gravel, he tensed. His opponent was on the little roadway then, creeping toward him, and sounding as if he might walk over the top of Slocum.

Just enough new-rising moonlight peeked above the trees and skylined the brute. Slocum recognized the man as one of the bigger older boys. He had no way of knowing how far off the other four were, but he couldn't risk letting this one through. He counted one, two more steps, then leapt to action. He drove the stock of the rifle at the big, shaggy head and was rewarded with the satisfying *thunk!* as wood met bone. The big man buckled in the moonlight, folding like a pocketknife before him. As he dropped, a groan wheezed from between his lips.

Great, thought Slocum. Now all I have to figure out is how to get him back to the barn and tie him up. Not one of my better-thought-out plans, but at least I prevented him from making his way to the house to torment the kids and the women.

But would he have tormented them? Maybe he was only trying to get away from his demented father, too. Maybe he was using the only thing he had at his disposal to do so—the darkness of nighttime. Or maybe the father's brainwashing was so complete that he was intent on doing them all harm, on stopping them any way he knew how.

Slocum tried to drag the brute off the road by the shirt collar, but between the man's size and his dead weight, Slocum's own injured leg, and trying to balance his rifle, he wasn't up to the challenge. He managed to get the big brute to the edge of the road. He also managed to unbuckle the man's gun belt. He slung the leather over his shoulder, making sure the pistol was secured with a hammer thong in its holster.

He figured he'd head back to the house, get someone's help, maybe Judith, then truss up the man and drag him to the barn before heading out to do the same to the others. It was just luck that this one fell in his lap, but maybe the men weren't all that bright and would keep making the same mistakes. He could only hope so.

He repeated his short journey to the house, where the women were still trading random shots with the unseen attackers. "They'll ease up once full dark lands on us. There's no way they can keep shooting with any accuracy in the dark. But that means no lamplight from inside here."

"Why, Mr. Slocum, you sound as though you've done this sort of thing before."

"Matter of fact, I have." But there was no time for his comment to sink in, because a fresh barrage of bullets chewed their way into the already pocked exterior of the little house. But something about it was different.

There were less of them from the front, which meant that some had moved or were in the process of skirting them, surrounding the place. None would be safe, then, for the inside of the house was half exposed to the weather. It sat there, open at the back, the dry wind slicing through, making slow progress in chewing away all the work some long-ago farmer and his family had put into the little place.

Bu he figured he still had enough time to truss up that big brute he'd coldcocked earlier, then drag him to the barn. "I'm going back out there. I have to deal with something." He didn't dare mention to them that he had clubbed one of their own. They'd either attack Slocum or find the man he'd hit and tear him to pieces. He felt sure that, given half a chance, they could be as crazy as their father. If Slocum felt himself doubting that fact, he only had to think back on what they did to the old man and the boys.

He slipped out and paused, low, behind the wagon. No shots rang out. Maybe they hadn't really begun surrounding them yet. He took the chance and headed low and as fast as he was able. No shouts. He'd made it to the far end of the barn when he heard a sound behind him. He spun fast, jacking a fresh round into play in the rifle.

Judith stared at him, her eyes wide. "Don't shoot me, Mr. Slocum," she whispered.

"Dammit, Judith, what are you doing? I almost . . ." He shook his head, then said, "Come on. I thought we talked about you following people. Bad habit, you know."

By the time he made it back with Judith in tow to where he had dropped the man like a big sack of wet sand, the man was gone. "I know I left him here," he said in a low whisper.

"Who?"

He looked at her. "I hit one of them." He saw the worried look on her face. "Nah, I mean I knocked him out, not shot him. Not yet."

"Well, he ain't here now, Mr. Slocum."

"Gee, thanks. Not sure what I'd have done without you along."

"No need to get huffy with me. I'm here, ain't I?"

"Yeah, so you are. Okay, but we best keep it down, skedaddle back to the house."

As Slocum and Judith light-footed back around the low barn, he heard the quick ratcheting sound of a hammer cocking back. In the sliver of a second that it occurred to him, he dragged Judith down to the dusty earth and lay atop her as best he could to shield her from anything that might kick up—like a bullet. At the same time, he marked the burst of flame where the rifle shot came from and directed two quick pistol shots straight at it. He was rewarded with the sharp strangled gurgle of someone shot in the throat. That's all he'll ever say again, thought Slocum, acutely aware that the girl with him was probably the dying man's sister.

He pushed away from Judith. "You okay?"

He saw her nod once in the pale new moonlight.

"I'm sorry, Judith. You know I had no choice. They may be your family, but they are behaving like wild dogs."

"I know." Her voice sounded raw, husky, the voice of someone about to cry. He supposed he couldn't blame her. Kin was kin, after all.

"Let's get back to the house. We have to talk with the others, form a plan. Something tells me we're in for a long night."

Once back inside, he was careful to keep his voice down for fear of frightening the children, who were sleeping in a pile in the corner. He didn't blame them. But there was too much commotion tonight for the rest of them to get any rest.

"Look, ma'am. We need to post a couple of sentries so they don't sneak up on us. They're like a pack of mad wolves, there's no telling what they'll do. We should have at least four on constant lookout. By my count there are four of them."

"Five," said the old lady, but she paused when Slocum didn't respond. Her face grew stony and sad, all at once, when he shook his head.

"Who was it, then?"

He shrugged. "No way for me to know."

"You didn't see who you shot?"

"Not in the dark, no. I'm sorry."

"Then how do you know you got anybody?" She sounded hopeful.

"There was no mistaking it, ma'am."

She turned to the girl. "Judith, is he speaking truthfully?"

"Yes, Mama. He did it to save me." Then the girl broke down, sobbed into her hands. No one made a move to comfort her.

The old woman's face became even more pinched. "It's not knowing which of my babies is gone. I never should have done this, never should have dragged you all out here. It's my fight with him, always has been."

Ruth barked a short laugh. "Your fault? Your fight? Who do you think has put up with them all these years? Don't you dare try to shoulder this blame all for your own. I wear it proudly. I'm a full-grown woman and so are they." She nodded toward the twins.

"And Judith." Ruth looked around, but Judith must have slipped outside. "Wherever she got to is pretty near it, too. And someday they will be." She nodded toward her sleeping children. "No, Mama. This is our fight and we ain't goin' back."

Slocum cut in. "Fine, now that we all agree that we're on the same side, what do you say we hammer out a plan to keep them from wearing us down before we can do it to them."

Within a minute, they had each chosen a direction to keep guard over, the mother taking the front, along with Ruth covering the east and rear, while the twins took the west and helped with the front and rear. Slocum felt he would be best suited making sure the perimeter of the place got a close look throughout the coming long hours of dark. "While I'm out there, I'll find Judith and send her back inside to help you cover the house, protect the children."

"Mr. Slocum, don't shoot any more of my babies."

He stared at the old lady for a moment, then stepped on out the door into the dark, keeping low and hugging the side of the house. He hoped like hell they could buy enough time to get them to daylight. And after that? he asked himself—and came up with no good answer.

15

Slocum headed straight out the back and kept going until he felt the longer grass of the sloping meadow brush his fingers. Then he cut west and soon found himself in the sparse undergrowth. He intended to continue in this manner until he circled wide enough that he could come up on the men from behind them at their camp, assuming they had made one.

It was turning cold, so he guessed they had backed away from the roadway enough to build up a campfire. Likely as not, they'd try to storm the place in the night, so he didn't want to venture too far away from the women and children, but he had to try something. Sitting still, like a lone duck on a small pond, wasn't something he was used to, leg wound or no.

Most of all, it gave him the chance to do something constructive and a way to work out his frustrations with this family—both sides. He held nothing against the women—they were trying to better their lot in life. It was obvious they had to get away. And the men? What sort of family opened fire on its fellow family members? He didn't feel too bad about shooting one already.

He felt the ground slope gradually away from him, and he did his best to avoid stepping on anything that might crackle and snap underfoot—not an easy task in the dark. A couple of times he made the mistake of setting his wounded leg down too heavily on a brittle branch or loose rock and froze, crouched low, hoping none of the Tinker men were nearby with a rifle swung his way.

The night had gone cool, but he'd worked up a sweat in the short amount of time he'd been walking. Then he stepped on another stick with his increasingly stiff and throbbing, tired leg. The crackle of twigs sounded to him like a series of forest-floor gunshots. He paused, frozen in place. Then the finicky cloud cover slid westward and revealed the three-quarter moon. It served to help him orient himself. He looked down and saw he'd been steadily edging toward a forty-foot drop that led down to the rough roadway. But it was a drop with no easy way to the bottom, unless he ventured another few hundred yards to either side.

Slocum bent his head back and breathed deeply. The cool night air felt good on his feverish, sweat-covered forehead. What was he doing? He was as crazy as them. He should crawl back to the little ramshackle barn, curl up in the hay, and wait for daylight, when the Tinker men would most probably begin their demented assault again.

But then he heard it, the faint but unmistakable sound of someone or something advancing on him. He couldn't count on the moon to save him twice—discovering the cliff was enough. But it would be the moonlight that would reveal to him whatever was advancing with barely veiled stealth.

Slocum spun and dropped all at once, bringing the rifle to bear as he landed prone, his feet hanging off the edge of the rocky precipice. He squinted into the gloom, back where he'd come from. There was a dark, hunched shape there, looking less like a rock than a man trying to look like a rock. Whoever it was didn't realize that rocks, especially large ones, rarely wobbled. Then the rock spoke.

"That you, Peter? It's Caleb."

Slocum thought about his next move for a moment. Maybe this would work out just right, and he could draw in the fool as if he were using a call on a turkey or grunting for a moose. "Yeah," he said in what he hoped was a sufficiently Peter-sounding tone.

"Well, come here. I seen you for a while now, looks like you did what Papa asked and figured out a way down there. He wants to get in that house, without no more blood being spilled, only if need be, he said. I . . . I don't know if I can follow through with his wishes."

The man was breathing hard and he advanced like a bear, on all fours. Slocum couldn't back up, and dashing to either side would show the man he was definitely not his brother. He'd have to wait him out. At least he had the advantage of his rifle, and he trained it on the big man.

"Peter, where you at? I can't see you no more, the moon's gone to hiding again."

"Here." Slocum grunted, trying to keep the bulky shape of the man in view as he shambled forward.

"It's one thing to shoot at them adobe walls, where you know Mama and the girls won't get hurt, but it's another when you start thinking how some of them could have been hurt by our shooting and we might never know, just keep on shooting at them like Papa said we had to. That ain't right. But I daren't say a thing to Papa. You know what he's like, right, Peter?"

The man had advanced to within twelve or so feet. Slocum was trapped with no direction to go but backward, off the forty-foot cliff. And that was no direction he wanted to travel.

"Peter? Why don't you say something? You don't think I'm wrong, do you? I thought we talked about all this, agreed we'd do what we could to keep the girls from harm, right? Peter?"

Slocum licked his lips, made a vague moaning sound as if Peter had been hurt. If Peter were the one he'd shot in the neck, then yes, Peter had indeed been hurt.

The man rose up off his hands to his knees, leaning slightly forward, facing Slocum. The clouds parted, revealing half of the moon, and offered just enough of its light to illuminate the scene before Slocum, as if God had lit an oil lamp just for them. Thanks, thought Slocum, as he watched the big angry face of one of the Tinker boys, the biggest of them all, from the looks of him, grow even angrier.

"You . . . you . . ."

Slocum raised the rifle, thumbed back the hammer, and the

big brute froze in mid-knee-stride. But his menacing scowl stayed on his face. He was within striking distance. Even if Slocum got off a shot, the man could probably succeed in pushing Slocum off the cliff. While it was not a hundred-foot drop, he'd fall backward, and with his leg, there wasn't much chance he'd come out of it in very good shape at all. Not to mention the fact that he'd probably not land on anything soft, just a hard-packed roadway or rocks at the sides of the road. No, it would do no good to have this brute drive him backward off the cliff.

"One more move, big man, and I'll drop you where you stand. I'll core your foul heart and you can meet up with your brother. You know, the one I already shot in the throat."

"What?" The man nearly bellowed where before they had talked in whispers. It had the effect Slocum had hoped for—it riled the beast. But then the man did something he'd not counted on . . . the brute swatted at the rifle. The shot went wide, a brief flash of flame and curling smoke filled their faces, the stink clouded their noses, and the blast felt like steel hammers ringing on anvils in their ears.

He came onto Slocum at a full-bore bull-grizz gallop, covering the last few yards at a bellowing lope. Slocum had just enough time to swing the rifle barrel hard at the man's face. It connected and the brute was, if only for a moment, stunned into silence. He swayed on all fours like a bear, shaking his head. Must have addled him. If Slocum hadn't been so preoccupied with trying to get away from the cliff top, where he'd slid farther off, his legs now hanging in space, he would have struck the man a second time in the head, but he found himself clawing his way back upward, realizing he was rapidly losing ground, sliding farther backward off the cliff top.

He let go of the rifle and managed to snag a hand on a thin, finger-thick sapling, but it soon pulled away from the thin topsoil, its roots popping and tearing. And then, just as it let go, Slocum's boot, the one at the end of his weakened, wounded leg, found solid purchase against an upthrusting of rock that felt solid enough to trust with his entire weight. By that time, the big man had regained some sense of coherence, and was groping along the ground, once again in darkness. That moon was playing the devil out of them tonight, thought Slocum.

He heard shouts from below in the roadway . . . men's voices.

"What's going on up there? That you, Peter? Caleb? Stop playing games. God don't approve of a game player!"

The old man railed on, from what sounded to Slocum like a position directly below them. He was thankful the moon was still covered up, but for how long, he had no idea.

The big man lunged at him again, and caught a handful of Slocum's shirt. He felt it tighten and the shoulder seams pop from the tightening grip of the big, work-hardened hand.

Try as he might, Slocum was growing weaker, scrabbling for his now-lost foothold, and in a position such that fighting back would render him completely at the man's power. And two feet from falling off the cliff.

He had one chance. Now or never, Slocum, old boy, he told himself. He reached up at the growling, chuffing face, got a handful of jowly cheek meat, and pressed his thumb into the man's eye socket.

"Gaaah!" the big brute wailed and lessened his grip on Slocum's shirt enough that he rolled out of the hold, at the same time grabbing a thicker tree his arm had slammed into seconds before. The rough bark at the base provided a welcome handhold. He swung his body upward and drove his wounded leg right into the bent brute's shoulder. The man grunted and Slocum did it again. The moaning man lashed out, trying to grab hold of him, groping blindly, wildly for Slocum. Then his hand found Slocum's rifle and he snatched it up, still shaking his head from the eye gouging.

"Oh no you don't," said Slocum through gritted teeth. He drove a fist straight at the man's nose and felt something inside it snap twice under his knuckles, then smear sideways into pulp. An immediate gush of blood, warm and foul, burst from the screaming man's face. Slocum followed it up with a boot heel to the middle of the man's mouth, and still he didn't let up. Slocum kept pushing, driving the big man backward. In his dazed condition, the man never noticed the cliff edge until it was far too late.

Slocum grew vaguely aware that the men's voices had carried on shouting up at them from down below.

As the man felt himself slipping backward off the cliff, he screamed unintelligible words, like the world's biggest baby howling and gibbering for help. But he kept sliding backward, his fingers scrabbling at the thin matte of topsoil, roots, and gravel, none of which offered a bit of help.

The man let go of the rifle and slid backward, back, back. Then the clouds drifted once again from the moon's face, and the two men looked each other in the eyes. Slocum had no more time for thought before the man, staring with shock at the other, dropped backward. Though it was only forty feet, he screamed like a man tumbling into a steep gorge. Then his voice cut off abruptly with a hard, smacking sound and Slocum knew the man was dead.

Drifting up to him from the base, Slocum heard at least two men's voices, but one was loud and howling and full of pious rage.

Slocum lay atop the cliff for fleeting seconds before he realized he had to move. They would be up here, he knew, within minutes. And he needed all the time he could muster to get away. He groped in the dark once again for his wayward rifle, cursing the fickle moon. He found it, and used it to drag himself upright, then took off at a low, panting lope back the way he had come. Back toward the broken-down homestead and the women.

Judith had said the old woman knew medicines. Maybe she could fix him up with something that would take away the ache he felt throughout his entire body. Otherwise, the only thing Slocum knew to fix how he felt was time. Time and sleep. He just wanted a bit of sleep.

He straggled back down the trail he'd made, shapes rising up then becoming rocks or fallen trees in the shifting light of the night sky. The filtered moonlight brightened patches of earth and revealed holes and jumbles of rocks just right for snapping an ankle. Slocum finally found himself at the edge of the wood and paused, but heard no sounds from behind. Still, by his count, there were three more of the bastards out there somewhere. They would be angry, but he didn't think the old man would give up now. Not after Slocum had killed two of his boys. As he staggered toward the little compound, it was strangely quiet, and he wondered what the old lady would think about the fact he'd been forced to kill another of her offspring. Not that he had any intention of telling her. At least not right away.

16

He'd grown so tired that by the time he staggered back toward the house, he hardly cared whether the place was overrun with crazy-eyed itinerant preachermen or big-breasted women toting rifles and shotguns and six-shooters. All he wanted was a drink of cool water and a nest in the old hay in a corner of the barn. He'd take his chances with anyone foolish enough to creep around in the dark. Tired or not, he could still squeeze the trigger on his Colt.

He was troubled by the fact that the men seemed to have an endless amount of ammunition. It must have come from that secret stash the women hadn't been able to break into. He still wanted to get to that camp of theirs—must be one back behind the small ridge they'd been firing from. If he saw that they had carried a decent amount of guns and ammunition, plus food and other gear, he'd know they were committed to this invasion.

If they didn't have much more than guns and bullets, then they had expected to overrun the women and drag them by the hair back to their farm. Either way, Slocum knew he had to get to their camp; it was just a matter of when. And he knew that answer: It would have to be tomorrow, because he couldn't go on. It had been one long day, then he'd been shot, then in a gunfight, then in a brawl with a big brute of a man atop a cliff. What next? He could only think of sleep.

He looked toward the house, saw a figure leaning by the back of the house in the moonlight. It looked like Ruth, or maybe one of the twins. He held up his arms. "Hey," he said. "It's me . . . Slocum. Just letting you know I'm back."

The woman turned to him and he saw that he'd been mistaken. It was the mother. She held the heavy shotgun in the crook of her arms and faced him.

"Did Judith make it back?"

"Yep, all my girl chicks are sleeping inside right now. Be nice to have all my children with me. And all of 'em going to California. See how the old bastard would like that."

He could say nothing, merely nodded. He was too tired to think straight.

The older woman broke his reverie with another question. "What was that shot I heard up yonder, a while ago, likely I heard some shouts, too. You know anything about it?"

"Might," he said. "Nothing of bearing right now. Ma'am, I am very tired. I will take my leave, and grab a few hours of sleep in the barn. Don't hesitate to yell and I'll come running." As he trudged back to the barn, he thought of the fact that he'd killed another of them. He wished he could be sure that the men wouldn't try any more barrages tonight. At least until first light. If he were a praying man, he thought, he'd ask for that favor.

He flopped back onto the hay and within seconds was snoring lightly. Scant minutes later, Slocum heard softer footfalls creeping along the outside of the barn, then at the edge of the open door, he saw the faint outline of someone holding a rifle waist-high. He hefted his Colt Navy and low-walked back into shadow, perfectly positioned to ambush the ambusher. Any second now, the person would come into view. One more step, another . . . He lashed out, silent as a stalking cat, and clamped a big hand on the intruder's mouth, knocking the rifle to the ground with his gun hand. It was a woman! He dragged her backward into the shadows.

"Which one are you?" He stood behind her, holding her close, his strong hands pinning her arms to her sides, though she lashed at him with her head, her hair whipping him in the face. He did his best to avoid her vicious backward kicks with her boots to his shins. "Ow! Dammit, who are you?" To her credit, she didn't yell, which told him she knew they were to keep quiet, knew the potential danger of attracting attention to themselves.

"It's Ruth."

He didn't release her just yet. "What were you doing, slinking around outside?"

"I wasn't slinking. I wanted to make sure you were all right. That's all. I . . . I never got to thank you for bringing Judith back to us."

It sounded like a load of road apples to him, but Slocum sensed she wasn't going to attack him. Besides, from what he could feel, she didn't seem to have any place to carry another weapon. She wasn't wearing much more than a thin cotton dress and her boots. He let go of her arms, and she stayed standing there in the dark, her back to him, breathing heavily.

Then she did a curious thing—she backed up even closer to him, pushing her soft backside into him. She reached around behind him and pulled his hips into her and held him tight, grinding into him. Despite the dire predicament they were all in that night, Slocum felt himself rising to her insistent ministrations.

He knew he shouldn't, knew somehow this was wrong. She was plenty old enough, had been fine the other night, but having just talked with the girl's mother made him feel odd about this. But soon, it was too much for him to resist. He reached around and grasped her full breasts with his hands, rubbing them, working them just as she worked him.

She fumbled with his belt buckle, the buttons on his jeans, and soon had his pants pried apart, all the while keeping her back to him. He reached down and lifted the short cotton dress. She wore nothing under it and it slid up high, revealing silky soft skin under his rough hands. Her breath came in short gasps and she guided him between her velvety cheeks and eased him into her, bending low before him. Her back curved before him and she kept backing up into him, away then toward, and as they did, he guided them to the barn wall so he might get a bit of leverage.

Soon they were moving together, then apart, faster and harder, their bodies sweating in the cool night air, the only sounds slight huffing noises as they worked away at each other. And all too soon, it seemed to Slocum, she stiffened, arching her back and holding her breath for a long time. Then she slid off him, moved away from him, leaving him with a job half finished. He had no time to think anything more of it, because seconds later she reappeared before him, her dress hoisted high, and wrapping her legs high around his waist, she once again impaled herself on him.

She did her best to avoid his leg wound, though at times she rubbed it accidentally and he stifled a groan of pain. He wondered briefly if her own grazed shoulder ached much, and he kept in mind not to touch her there.

She felt different to him than she had the other night, sadder maybe. In the dim moonlight glowing in the interior of the little barn, he saw tears on her cheeks and knew he was right. Sad, no doubt, for her dead brothers, for the wrong turn their grand adventure had taken, for their miserable lives under the brutal hand of the crazy old man who'd fathered her.

From the way she worked at him, this was something she needed to do. So, he reasoned, should I be nothing less than obliging? Slocum resumed his task with vigor, feeling for the best handhold on this woman who seemed determined to use him to work out her frustrations, if not work him to death. Worse ways to go, he thought. And then he felt a tongue lick his ear and he saw her dark eyes stare into his, saw a smile on her face as she pressed herself against him.

He had no idea where he got his second wind from, nor how long it might last, considering the long day's events and injuries, but there was no way he could let this poor woman down. Maybe it was some sort of heavenly payment for all the hardships he'd been through on account of this family.

17

What felt like an eternity later—a blissful eternity—Slocum lay back in the hay once again, and he didn't awaken until he heard glass rupture and spray inward. His Colt Navy appeared in reflex born of long-honed instinct, in his hand as if conjured, and he swung his wounded leg, still stiff, outward. Someone had shot out the one last pane of glass in the barn's window. Whoever had built the place were a thoughtful bunch, as glass was dear enough in cost for a house, let alone a stable. Now that bit of finery had been obliterated.

It was still dark, but he felt rested enough that he knew it had to be close to dawn. Before he could crawl over to the window, the old man's voice rang out loud and clear—close enough for Slocum to pick out every word.

"The Lord saw fit to give me sons to continue His wonderful work, but then He saw fit to let the thieving women, them she-devils, spout flame and foul hatred and lay low two of my boys, my dear boys!" Another shot rang out, chipping off the house, from the sounds of it.

Slocum heard the sudden screams of frightened children from inside the house, then just as quickly heard women's voices shushing them.

"I ain't questioning the Almighty's wisdom in these matters, but I am wondering just what can be done about it." The old man continued to rant. "I prayed on it all night, you hear me, you vile witches! I prayed on it all night long!"

Slocum belly-crawled to the main doorway and took off his hat, then he peeked around the frame, cheek to the ground. The dull gray glow of early dawn would soon give way to lavender, then the blue of a new day. But for the moment, shadows were discernible again. Slocum held his spot. Odds of him being seen down low like this were slim to none.

He squinted toward the opposite side of the road, the high ground controlled by the men. But their number was, by the old man's admittance and Slocum's relative assurance, whittled down to three of their original five. The old man would be dangerous; the other big brute of a boy would be a danger, too. But the youngest? The slender boy, Luke, what of him? Slocum had to assume that he also knew how to wield a firearm, as it would seem even the girls had been taught how to do so.

Unless they taught themselves when the old man and his sons weren't watching, though that seemed unlikely. But the slender young boy had been trying to warn Slocum that day he'd found them. He bet the boy could still be saved, if that was the right word to use in this situation.

He seemed innocent enough that Slocum hated to lose him to a bullet. Then another shot whanged off a rock in front of the house.

They'd tried to sneak around the back of the place last night, but apparently Slocum had foiled those efforts. Was the old man trying to outflank them once again before he would lose the element of surprise that the near darkness of dawn could give him? These shots could be a distraction, though the speech sounded real enough.

He'd seen nothing moving out front, no sign of the old man, his voice echoing off the blunt stone of the house enough that Slocum wasn't sure just where the old crazy man was positioned. Still safe behind one of those roadside boulders, no doubt.

"I aim to drive you snakes out of your den! You will slither out of that house before I am through, or I will bring it down around you, stone by stone, that is a promise. And I do not speak of this lightly! It came to me in a vision in the night. The Lord whispered to me and told me what I must do."

There was a long pause. Slocum was sure the women were about to shout something of their own in response. He half smiled at the thought of what it might be, especially if Ruth had her way.

But Old Man Tinker chimed in again. "The Lord God Almighty also said that I was to give you witches one more chance to see the light of truth. In order to save your souls and your lives . . . and those of your children . . ."

Slocum recognized the sound of a honeyed tongue trying to slide guilt into the foolishness the old man was speaking.

"I say again, if you don't choose to save the lives of your children, you will have no one but yourselves to blame. But if you do cling to the hope that I am offering you by way of God's grace, then you may come on home, bound, of course, so that you devils might not claw my eyes out. For they are the very eyes that see the truth where you only see lies and evil. And then you can earn your place in my household once again. After a sufficient time of penance, of course."

"You better shut your foolish mouth, old man! We ain't going nowhere but away from you! You wad that book of yours up tight and—"

Slocum guessed that the old woman shut Ruth up before she had a chance to finish her choice suggestion to the old man.

"Demons! Devils! Harpies! Witches! You will all burn in the hellfires of eternity!"

As the man shouted, Slocum made his way to the other end of the barn and peered through a gap in the boards near the ground. It afforded him a close-up view of the Appaloosa's front legs. Apparently the horse was waiting for hay.

"Ain't gonna happen, fella. Go graze—but don't get shot or stolen." He didn't dare bring the horses into the barn. They'd turned all five horses back into the corral last night for fear of the barn being burned. The little paddock kept them close behind the barn, and was relatively protected from most directions the old man would be likely to attack from. And he didn't see anything that might be a man moving back there.

18

Other than random rifle shots that continued to pock the building, they heard nothing more from the man for the long hours of the day. The sun's heat bore down on them, cooking anything in its path. By midday, everything had grown hazy, hot to the touch, and uncomfortable. The old woman had mixed up a poultice for Slocum's leg wound and it helped ease the swelling and numbed the throbbing pain of it. He reluctantly accepted a crate to sit on in a shady spot in the house.

By the time dark began to fall, Slocum had regained much of his strength and was grateful that the corner of the house most protected for the frontal assault was the cooking area set up by the old woman. She really knew how to feed a big brood. Slocum watched in amazement as she made barely a few handfuls of cornmeal and a small pot of beans into a meal for them all. He refused, knowing their supplies were limited, but brought his own in from his bags in the barn.

He felt less guilty about taking a second cup of coffee. The old woman didn't want his supplies, but he insisted, and he could see the relief on her face. But it was fleeting. He was sure she was dwelling on the old man's shouts. And though she probably suspected Slocum of killing a second of her boys, she knew, too, that most of them had slung plenty of return lead in the frequent volleys last night.

"Any chance of talking him out of his crazy plans?"

Ruth shook her head and watched Judith playing with the kids. Some of them were Ruth's kids, but how many, Slocum didn't know. It didn't seem to matter to any of them anyway. One of the twins helped her mother clean up the dishes while the other kept watch out the back. Slocum kept an eye on the front, along with Ruth.

"That's just the thing, John, he's genuinely crazy," said Ruth. "Has been for a long, long time. That's why we have to get away from him."

The old lady came up, drying her hands on her apron. "Look, Mr. Slocum, you have to do me a favor."

He swore he almost saw a smile on her face.

"Well, I'll gladly listen to what you have to propose. That much I can do, and maybe more, should the idea strike me as useful to our situation."

She looked peeved, and said, "You've killed at least one of my boys, least you can do is help me save one of them."

"I'd like nothing better than to do that, ma'am. What do you have in mind?"

"It's Luke. He's a good boy. It pained me to have to leave him with them, but he's right at that age, he'll turn on a dime and side with them. But I can tell in his eyes he don't really know why he's doing it. Was that way when we commenced to whuppin' on his pappy and the other boys that day we left. Wouldn't listen to me none. The plan had been to take him with us, but by God, he fought like a wild thing, before the tincture took hold, that is."

"Tincture?" Slocum had no idea what she was on about.

"How else do you think we got them all to let us tie them to the fence?" Ruth winked at him. As she turned back to the window, she said, "Should have tied them tighter. At least that one out there, should have tied him around his neck."

The old woman darted past Slocum and slapped Ruth on the cheek. "He may be insane, he may have been a poor father, he may have been and still is a lot of things that ain't very good, but he is the man I love—or did once. He wasn't always this way. If you want to talk about him in such a way, you do it out of earshot of the little ones. And me, too."

Backed as he was to the crumbling old whitewashed wall, there was little Slocum could do. He was trapped between the two women who stared hard at each other, their angry bosoms working up and down inches from him. Yes, he decided, he felt very uncomfortable.

"Ladies, this is not the time nor place for this. We have to keep away from these windows and get ourselves ready to move out."

"Move out?" said the old woman. "Just how do you propose we do that? Ain't no way to leave, with us being pinned down here by him. It's not like we can jump on a horse and gallop on out of here."

"I'm working on that. Now as I see it, we have three of them, by Tinker's own admittance. If we could lure them in—"

"How?" one of the twins chimed in.

Slocum sighed. "I'm getting to that, Angel."

"I'm Mary."

"Oh, fine, Mary." Slocum looked at the twin. Hard to believe she was one of a set. "Where was I?"

"You mean before you got lost down Mary's dress?" Ruth snorted and peeked back out the window.

All three women, and Judith, too, smiled at him, and once again, he felt himself redden. "Okay, okay, back to the luring . . ."

But he didn't have the chance to say anything more because the old man fired another round, then began shouting again.

"You witches in the house! You have run out of time. The Lord has instructed me to burn you out!"

So there it was, thought Slocum. About time the old fool thought of it. He'd expected that threat for a whole day now.

The old woman turned to Slocum. "He wouldn't dare! There are children here . . ."

Ruth snorted again. "Dare? Course he dares. He hates us and wants us dead. And the sooner the children hear the truth, the better off they'll be. He's an evil bastard with a heart of stone." She held up a long finger in front of her face and said to her mother, "And you better think twice before you lay a hand on me ever again. You're part to blame in all this."

"Enough of this foolish bickering!" Slocum hissed. "If any of them get close enough with a torch, we have to stop them." He looked hard at them. "We have to wing them, you understand? Or a leg wound. Enough to stop them, but not kill them. They're too far away to throw a torch from the other side of the road."

And they waited. And waited. But no torches were thrown at them, no flaming arrows. Perhaps it had been a bluff. Maybe they didn't even have a campfire. No matter, every minute without fire tossed their way was another minute of relative safety for them all.

Slocum went back to the barn in hopes of broadening their sight line. The horses were all still there, clustered close by the barn, not bothered by the occasional shouts or shots. Amazing what they get used to, he thought. He remembered the cavalry horses in the war. After a while, they seemed to grow accustomed to the cannon fire and screams of dying men. Maybe, he thought, like men, they just grew emotionally deadened to it.

19

Tunk Mueller still rode northward a day after he'd creased the hide of whoever had tried to ambush him, he hoped for good, but somehow he knew that particular wish wasn't to be. And the more he thought about it, the more it ate at him. Who would be dogging him and why? He'd no doubt left plenty of folks plenty of reasons over the years to pester him. But he hoped he would be able to come across this latest one and finish the job he'd started.

He was about to stop the horse once again, give himself time to think this thing through, when he saw a string of smoke in the distance, down along the barren flatland of the valley below. In the breezeless sky, the smoke rose straight up. That fire could mean food, and food could mean drink. And drink, Mueller decided, could mean people with money saved up. A cash box or at least a coin purse. "Hmm," he grunted and reached into his saddlebags for the last of his whiskey, confident that he would soon be experiencing the splendors of someone else's drink.

As he rode, he swallowed back the dank brown gargle. It tasted of tree roots and urine, but it sure, by God, gave a man a reason to open his yawp and growl. He belched long and low and looked down at his hole-filled undershirt. It was once red, but had in the past week on the trail made the journey to mostly

107

brown, with some sooty streaks to break up the monotony. But it was the bear-cub growling of his empty gut that drew his attention.

"I know, I know. I'd hoped to feed you by now." He patted his belly. "It is an almighty embarrassment to me that I am unable to feed myself and my horse properly." He said this to the air around him, flashed a glance at the still-far-off smoke at the edge of the forest. "I wish I'd turned out differently than how Pap said I'd turn out. If I hadn't been clouted and clopped on the ears for everything I did wrong, I might have become a man of means and high taste."

He upended the bottle and glugged the last of it down, regarded the empty green-tinged glass bottle, and leaned far back in his saddle and let 'er fly. The thing arced high. He tried to follow it, but he lost it briefly in the sunlight, then it reappeared, whipping end over end, and landed with a *tunk*. The sound was satisfying and brought a smile to his face.

"You gonna to miss that bottle, if'n I was to retrieve it?"

Mueller's eyes flew wide open and he whipped his head back and forth. "What in the hell was that?" Even the horse ceased its relentless plodding and cast a glance sideways.

"Mister?"

Tunk looked down and not twenty-five feet to his left stood a thin, dirt-covered boy of perhaps fourteen. He wore filthy sacking fashioned into some sort of long garment cinched in the middle with what looked to Mueller like a root.

Tunk snatched up his pistol, cocked it, and aimed at the boy. "Who are you and where did you come from?"

"Aw, don't shoot me, mister. I ain't done nothing wrong."

The kid seemed not half as perturbed at having a gun drawn on him as having someone think him a thief.

"I ask you again, and I am not a man known for his patience. Where in the blue blazes did you come from?"

"I was just out here looking for something to eat. That's our camp down yonder." He nodded at the smoke, toward which Mueller had been riding.

"You said 'our'—that mean you got family?" Mueller regarded the boy.

"Yes sir, that I do. Got me a pappy and a mammy and a baby sister. All of us is camped, waiting for someone with a horse or wagon to haul us on out of here."

The kid looked at Mueller, but didn't say much more. He didn't need to. Mueller understood. "Let me get this straight. You all are waiting out here in this god-awful hot summer sun, waiting on someone to yarn you on out of here?"

The kid nodded as if what Mueller was asking made all the sense in the world. "That's 'bout the size of it, yes sir. You come on down, I'll be able to show you real hospitality, you mark my words."

"Does that involve food?"

The kid paused long enough to scratch his head. "If we had enough food to fill our bellies, do you think I would have been out here roaming the hillside for a bite of anything at all?"

"What do you eat, boy?"

He seemed not to hear Mueller. His smiling eyes had gone glassy. "We're nearly dead around here."

Tunk stopped his horse. "You all haven't been afflicted with some sort of disease, have you?" He leaned from his horse, squinting at the boy.

The boy moved closer.

"No, no you don't. You keep your distance. I aim to keep mine."

The boy chuckled, a tired, hollow sound. "I ain't sick, not yet anyway. But I keep gnawing green bark, I will be."

"How old are you?"

"I'm nearly sixteen."

"God, you'll pardon me for saying it, but you look younger than that."

The boy said nothing and they kept moving toward the smoke. Though it was still some distance away, they had drawn near enough that Mueller could make out a couple of shapes stretched out near the fire. Could be his folks, thought Mueller.

"What happened to you and your kin that put you in such hard straits?"

"We was rolling along in our wagon, doing our best to get to California. Pappy heard there was a new gold strike and he aimed to get hisself a piece of it."

"That so?" Mueller tucked away that thought. Information like that might prove useful down the road.

"Yes sir. Pappy's right fond of gold. He ain't got much but . . ."

"Go on."

"Look here, it's that bottle." The boy retrieved it, unbroken, from beside a hummock of grass. "That's lucky."

"I never said I was fixing to give up that bottle, boy." Mueller scratched his chin.

"But you threw it away."

"I threw it, yes. But away? Not hardly."

The boy turned the bottle over in his grubby hands, then held it up to Mueller. The man ignored the gesture and kept the horse walking forward. The swish of grass and the light clomp of the horse's hooves were the only sounds for another few minutes.

"You see," said Tunk. "We often play a game, me and the horse. I will chuck that there bottle far along the trail, in the direction we are headed, and when we come on up to it, why, that horse will pick it up in his teeth as gingerly as you please, and hand it on up to me."

The boy smiled, his teeth brown nubs in his tight-skinned face. "You're funnin' me. Show me. Show me how that horse can do such a trick." He handed the bottle up to Tunk.

But Tunk shook his head. "Naw, we're almost to your camp. Don't want to go clunking anybody in the bean. Another time."

The boy looked disappointed and rubbed the bottle, but perked up again right away. "You wanna stay for supper?"

"Supper? Why, boy, you said you didn't have no food."

"I never did."

"About close to that, though. Hell, you look like you could eat . . ." He was going to say a horse, but he didn't want to give the kid any ideas.

"Oh, we got food to eat, don't you worry none. Mammy won't mind."

Mueller's brow wrinkled, but he said nothing. The boy was so thin, there was less than no chance that they had food enough for themselves, let alone to feed a stranger. Then his nose wrinkled, too. What in God's name was that hard smell? It seemed to hang right there in a ring around the little camp, like a kill gone off and green with age.

As he dismounted, well outside the camp, the boy went on ahead to the smoldering campfire and laid on another couple of thin sticks. "Mammy? Pappy? This fella here is come for supper." He smiled at Tunk.

Tunk caught sight of a small rock pile about as long as his leg. Stuck at one end were two sticks lashed into a rough cross with a strip of leather thong.

"That's my sister," the boy said, following Tunk's gaze. "She's still resting up. She's powerful tired most all the time."

"I should say," said Tunk to himself, eyes wide. Then he raised his voice. "Where's your wagon, boy? Stock?"

"Gone, they done took 'em all."

"Who?"

"Oh," he sighed as if he were tired of telling the story. "It was them who raided us a long time back. Bad things happened then, took all we had." He looked out over the waving grasses, flat as far as Tunk could see. "I was off on my own." He waved an arm in no real direction. "Trying to find us some tubers. Mammy's partial to such things."

He looked around himself, at his parents, the grave, the smoking fire, and little else. Finally his gaze rested on Tunk and his voice was quieter. "But when I come back, there wasn't much left but my family. But that's what matters, right? That's what Mammy always says."

Tunk didn't say anything.

The boy was smiling down at the figures laid along the fire, unmoving as if they were in a deep snooze. His parents were wrapped in holey wool blankets and hides with patchy hair, buffalo or bear, Tunk wasn't sure. They lay unmoving, not even waking up or looking his way. He had a god-awful bad feeling creeping up the back of his head. Something wasn't right, but he couldn't figure out what it was.

As the boy stepped over one of them, his bare foot caught an edge of a blanket and peeled it off what appeared to be skinned legs of a person.

"What you got under there, boy?" Tunk narrowed his eyes, but didn't step any closer.

"Oh, that?" The boy bent and lifted free the rest of the blanket. "That's just Pappy. He don't say much nowadays. Been a hard trip on him."

Tunk Mueller had seen a whole lot of rank things in his life—a good many of them he'd done while others were the leavings of scavengers, both human and animal. But this beat them all to hell.

The boy's pappy, or what was left of him, had flopped backward, arms by his sides and a sort-of-smile on his skin-bone face. The rest of him, though, looked about like how a bear carcass would resemble after a week or two of a campful of hungry miners eating off it. Mostly bone and sinew and bits of muscle, all dried a puckery brown. Only this body had been a man and the one doing the eating was his boy. In fact, Tunk could see some resemblance, particularly in the thinness of them both.

"He's nearly finished," said the boy, still smiling, as he pointed to his father. "But Mammy's still in good shape." Before Tunk could stop him, the boy whipped back the other blankets and skins. A swarm of agitated blueflies rose up and clouded the air before working their way back down again to their task, feasting on what was left of the dead woman.

Mueller turned away, his lips puckered while he worked to breathe through his mouth. That would explain the smell, he thought. Raw carcass.

"I'll be right back," said the boy cheerfully from behind him. "Fetch us some tubers."

"Yeah," said Tunk as he caught sight again of the small rocky grave not far away. Must have started with his sister. He had heard of people doing such things, but never thought he'd run into them. The desolate landscape, he had to admit, did not appear to offer much promise in the way of finding food. Tunk heard himself whispering something his mother had said so long ago: "You do with what you got at hand."

He looked back, but the boy was walking away, a large skinning knife in his hand, the blade crusted with dried blood and hunks of gristle. Then Tunk saw something curious. A thin bit of sunlight worked through the gloom and he caught sight of a faint gleam in the sagged mouth of the boy's father.

Tunk stepped closer, saw the boy was a ways off in the grass, digging at something. Tunk slid out his own sheath knife, used the blade tip to push open the dead man's mouth even wider. What few teeth the man had left were blackened and full of holes—except for two gold ones in the back, one on either side on the bottom.

Well, thought Tunk. This old boy is past needing such fine and valuable choppers. I expect he won't miss them. He slid the knife in there and pried at one of them. It soon popped out and Tunk caught it with the blade tip just before it dribbled down the man's dried gullet.

Far behind him, Tunk heard the boy grunt as if from exertion, and turned to see the boy lunging at him. The thin youth had that crusted-blade knife that looked to be half the length of his arm, and it looked to the man as if he was fixing to stick it into Tunk, sure as sugar is sweet. But the boy was weak and slow.

It seemed to Tunk, just before his boot connected with the boy's ribs and he heard that cracking sound, like fresh dry twigs make when you toss them on flame, that the boy knew he was in a poor state. Tunk could see it in his eyes. Almost like he was grateful for the kick.

The blow sent the kid sprawling backward. His strange little rag of a dress had flapped upward and Tunk saw that the boy's parts were as shriveled as the rest of him. The kid lay there, not moving, except for his slowly rising chest.

"Get up, boy. We got to have us a talk. What's been going on here ain't right, and you know it. Just my bad luck I come upon you when I did. I'd say you need to figure out a better way to live." He approached the boy with care, one hand on the butt of his pistol, his own long knife still gripped in his hand. "Maybe you could follow me. I'm aiming for California. Could be I'll shoot a deer now and again, give you a haunch and a place at the campfire. But you got to leave these heathen ways behind, you understand?"

The boy said nothing. Tunk stood over him. "Boy?" He toed

the lad's leg. Nothing. He noticed the boy's chest wasn't rising anymore. Then he saw the thin stream of blood leaking out from under the boy's chest. He flipped over the thin body with his boot tip and there was the knife, half sunk in the boy's back.

"Aw, now how in the hell did you manage that, boy?"

The kid's eyes were half open, still glassy, and his mouth was sagged. Tunk regarded him for a moment, then pulled the knife out of the boy's back, tossed the knife onto the grass, and rolled him once again onto his back. He walked to the nearly dead fire, retrieved the empty bottle from where the boy had stood it upright, and laid it on the boy's chest. It rolled off and caught in his arm, like you'd hold a puppy or a baby.

"You keep that pretty bottle," said Tunk.

Then he went back to the boy's father's corpse and resumed his work on the man's last gold tooth. But he kept an eye on the dead boy, lest he was playing possum.

A few minutes later, Tunk Mueller looked about the shabby little camp, at the two dead adults, the one child's grave, and the boy he had had to kick, dead but bleeding out his last into the rough grass of the flat. He mounted the dun and reined the horse back toward where he'd come from.

He felt sure if he was to stay on this trail much longer, he was going to end up like these sad fools. No sir, this was a sign, as sure as the sun burned a man's brains and the moon chilled them, this was a sign. He had to head on back and track down whoever it was who'd been dogging him, make sure they were good and dead. It was the only way he felt sure he could prevent himself from ending up like this sad kid and his family. Had to be. After all, he'd been given a sign, plain as day.

20

From the barn, Slocum peered through the window in the south wall. He tugged his hat low and scanned the dark; barely a moonlit scene was visible. It appeared nobody needed shooting, thankfully. And as he mused on what to do next, his normally razor-sharp reflexes let him down: He never heard the footsteps behind him.

He winced as a series of quick slaps lashed at his face. A voice close by trembled with whispered rage. "You kilt my baby. I won't let you do it again."

It was the old lady, understandably still fretting about whoever it was he'd shot earlier. "I reckon you'd rather have lost Judith or one of the other girls to a bullet then?"

"That ain't fair and you know it. Here," she said, "I brung you a cup of coffee. Getting cooler out here. Got to keep you alert."

"Thank you." He took the tin cup, hot to the touch, and blew and sipped. It was scalding—and good. "Have a seat," he said, and sat down on the straw. She slumped down next to him, leaned her shotgun against the wall.

"So . . . how's Ruth's arm?"

"Oh, she'll be fine. Just grazed. The blood stopped before it started."

He nodded, sipped.

She resumed talking, as if to herself, not seeming to care whether he heard her or not. It seemed to Slocum she just needed someone to listen to her, and who wasn't anyone in her family. "I had hoped that at least my youngest boy, Luke, might have come around, had not wanted to hurt his own mama." She dragged a hand across her eyes, used the hanky in her cuff to clear her tears. "I did a disservice to my offspring. I've been a fool. Once upon a time, I believed in that man. Then for far too long after that, I believed I could still trust him, that the man I once loved was still in there somewhere. But God got in the way."

She faced him. "He didn't used to be this way, Mr. Slocum. Used to be a good man. We was headed west years ago, Ruth was just a shaver, and her brother, Peter, was little more than that. We were headed to California to join up with my sister, Violet, and her husband and kids. They'd opened a mercantile, said there was plenty of opportunity for us out there. We only had but the two young'uns ourselves, so travel wasn't so much work as it is now. Also, we were young and full of ourselves, full of promise that thinking of the future holds."

"What changed your plans? Lots of folks make it to California every year."

"We broke down, just about like we are here." She shook her head at the irony of it all. "Only then, a gang of religious nuts, Bible-thumpers all, they come onto us, wormed their way into our heads—mine, too, I will admit. But you got to understand, Mr. Slocum, we was poor, and they were offering us a helping hand. Well, we figured, if this kindliness come bundled in a bit of the old Bible, how bad could it be? We figured we'd stay long enough to fix up the wagon, then we'd move on."

"But . . ." said Slocum, sipping the piping hot coffee. It was bitter, had a funny little bite to it, but it warmed him inside and for that he was thankful.

"Wasn't long before the whole Godly community was doing this and that for us, making us feel beholden to them more and more all the time. Before long, we were paying them for land, settin' up the farm."

"Oh, I see," said Slocum.

She nodded. "That ain't the half of it. They told us we were going to have the first house because we were the last ones to join up with them. I told Rufus that didn't make no sense no how, and that I wanted to get to California."

"But . . ." said Slocum again. This woman was surely a talker once she warmed to her subject.

"But my husband, Rufus, he was always a bit of a soft touch, soft in the head when it come to such matters. Easily persuaded, if you know what I mean. He said it all made sense to him and that I shouldn't be so selfish. Said I was shaming him in front of the congregation." She looked at him and Slocum could see the twinkle in her eyes of the woman she used to be. Young, vivacious, pretty, and ready for a full life in California, the land of promise to so many.

"Hell," she continued. "The only shameful thing about those thumpers was that they up and left in the night, took most everything of value we had. Left us with land that thankfully nobody has come along and said they own, a Bible that has caused my family more harm than good, and a husband who never did figure out how to take in the true meaning of the words in that book. I'm not even sure he knows how to read all that well, truth be told. Just kept making up meanings to suit his whims."

"I know what you mean, ma'am. Some folks are born to lead, some to follow, some just can't seem to figure out which direction they should head in and end up dithering away their days."

She nodded. "So all through the years, I kept up a correspondence with my sister in California. But whenever he could, Rufus would take the letters and burn them, make me watch. Wasn't but a letter a year, sometimes two, if we was lucky. But he claimed it was devil's work and that California was a sinkpit of sin and degradation. Those are his words, not mine."

"So you'd still like to go there?"

"I would, yessir. And I got that last letter from my sister in San Francisco, invited me like she always done through the years to join her. Around that time, things got bad betwixt the boys and Rufus and me and the girls. I don't need to tell you what will happen betwixt boys and girls of a certain age. I'm to blame, bad things had happened among the older children, living alone like this out in the hills, no strangers in months and months at a time, nowhere to run off to, a father like as not to kill you, bullwhip you for talking askance at the dinner table . . . I just couldn't bear knowing that my two youngest might end up tainted in some way, too. Little Judith and young Luke. He's a good boy, Mr. Slocum, I wish you could meet him."

"I believe I did," said Slocum, sipping more coffee. "And you're right, he is still a good lad. Just needs to get off on his own in the world before—"

"Yes," she said. "Before Rufus taints him like all the rest, mostly with his talk of God and the Bible, all good in their own place, but not in the way he preaches it."

"What about your sister's husband? What sort of a man will he be to you?"

She laughed. "Not much of one—he died not long after we got sidetracked out in this hellish place. I can't call what we did settling, 'cause that never set right with me, all these years I knew I'd be moving on one day, with or without him. As the years went by, it became obvious that it would be without him. Now I'm glad of it. His religion is so twisted in his mind that it made him value men, his own sons, over anything else. Said he wanted only grandsons. Daughters and granddaughters, he said, were cattle, only good for making more men. No, I don't call them my sons no more. Can't think of them that way. They're lost to me. Just like him. They're adults who make up their own minds."

"But under his influence," said Slocum, "they'll never get a chance to make up their own minds."

She was silent for a long minute, brooding, he knew, on a past largely wasted and on a life that could have been. And this reminded him why he was what he'd heard once called a "freebooter," someone who roamed, living a life that, to the best of his ability, harmed few others and mostly was not a life full of regret. Though he figured that at the end of his days, a little regret might not be a bad thing. It meant that there were more things he wanted to do that he just hadn't gotten to yet.

"My sister runs a boardinghouse in San Francisco, says she's very successful, mostly rents rooms to traveling businessmen.

Says she's got nice velvet drapes in the drawing room, lovely bedrooms, enough for all the girls." The old woman looked at him, an odd smile on her mouth. "Says she rents rooms to men who don't expect to be around for long-term visits."

Slocum wrinkled his brow. He caught himself just short of saying that it sounded to him like her sister was a madam, but she beat him to it.

She let out a low, whispered cackle. "I know exactly what she's up to, Mr. Slocum. And I'll be glad to take her up on the offer of expanding the business, keep it in the family." She winked. "After all, we might as well get paid to do what they been doing all these years. And that way, I can make sure no one harms my girls." She hefted her shotgun. "I reckon I can do that all right. I don't mind saying that I am a crack shot. And if it's something they don't wanna do, they don't have to. But at least they'll have a home. I can help set them up, maybe even get them educated. They could all be ladies of the world."

"Well," said Slocum. "The world will literally be right at your feet, with the docks. But beware of the Barbary Coast. It's a rough section you'd all do well to avoid."

"You sound like you been there, Mr. Slocum." She winked.

"Yes, ma'am, a time or two." He winked back.

She laughed and stood slowly, joints popping in protest, and used the shotgun as a prop. "Time to get back in there." Then she patted his shoulder and left the barn. He heard her footsteps receding, and despite how he felt, he wished she would keep quieter, sure that she was not heeding his earlier advice of staying low and staying put, keeping watchful. As if she no longer cared what happened to her. As if she'd given up.

21

Minutes after the old woman left him, already weak from a long day filled with leg pain, hardship, and hard exercise, Slocum slipped like a sack of wet sand to the straw. Try as he might to fight it, the day wore on him and he fell into a deep doze.

Hours later, how many he had no idea, Slocum awoke slowly, groggy and fuzzy headed, as if he'd been on a three-day drunk. It was still dark. He tried to sit up, but found he was hog-tied, his knees drawn up to his chest, his hands lashed around his shins, all tied tight, and his leg throbbed like cannon fire.

Beside him sat Judith.

"What in the hell is going on here? Who tied me up?"

"Shhh!" she hissed. "You wanna get us kilt?"

"Frankly, I don't really care what happens to you or yours. You've all cost me time and flesh. And I'm sick of it. Untie me now!"

Judith lay low, leaned out of the door frame, in the same position he'd been in hours before. "They're doing it!" she gasped.

"Doing what?" he said, louder than he intended.

"Quiet, Mr. Slocum, you want them to find us?"

"Yes. I have no desire to be trussed up. Now what are they doing?" He noticed a flickering light through the gaps in the barn boards to his right and scooted sideways. He peered through the gappy boards and saw a flaming torch making its way down the rock face across the road.

"They're going to torch the house, dammit. Judith, cut me loose!"

"No, you'll shoot whoever's bringing the torch."

"Yeah, unless we can find some other way to stop them before they get close enough to throw it."

She looked at him. "But that's what Mama doesn't want. She doesn't like your plan of shooting them. She has her own plan."

"Oh, great. What has she come up with?" He struggled with the wraps, but he was bound fast, and his hands throbbed as the ropes cut into them from his struggling.

"You'll see." Judith leaned back out the door frame, watching.

"Untie me, dammit. This is foolish."

"No, Mama says you're too good, you'll try to do the right thing and that will end up killing more family or them killing you, and none of us want that." She looked at him briefly in the dark, then leaned back out around the door frame.

Slocum turned back to the gaps in the boards. "You be careful, don't lean out too far. I don't trust them."

The old man began shouting as the torchbearer stepped onto the road. "You devils! You demon spawn! You have earned this! Every second of it! As your bodies begin to roast, you will scream and God Himself will not help you! You are beyond redemption! I have tried my best to save your doomed souls, but you have made your beds, you demons! You shall perish in the flames of hell! And Luke will deliver the death blow! He will prove himself a man and the heavens shall sing his name into the Book of Life!"

"What in the hell is he going on about?" Slocum shifted tighter to the wall, pressing his eye closer to the boards, forgetting for a moment the hard bindings of the ropes. He couldn't see the old man, who was still hidden well away in the safety of the dark and under cover of rocks and trees and night.

And then down came the boy, Luke, his skinny arm raised

above his head, the flaming torch held high, lighting his face. His eyes squinted against the heat and glare. He stopped at the edge of the road, and with his other hand resting on the butt of his side arm, he stood still, looking at the little ruined house.

His mother came out into the rubble-filled dooryard, a lantern held aloft, mimicking her young son's posture. "That you, Luke? Sweet boy, you come to see your mama. Finally come back to me?"

Slocum heard the old woman's voice catch in her throat. The boy, Slocum saw even at that distance, stood still, trembling.

From behind him, the old man roared, "Boy! Don't you listen! She is a devil woman! Devil woman! She will kill you and pull you down into the cauldron of hell, where your soul will suffer eternal torments, boy! Get walking, walk on and throw that fire! Do as God bids you!"

The boy still stood, quaking and staring forward. He glanced back once over his shoulder, wincing every time his father lashed him with another layer of Biblically tinged insult. Then he looked again at his mother. Finally he reached forward with his gun hand, empty of any gun, and his thin, trembling fingers groped outward as if beckoning his own mother to him. He took one, two tottering steps forward.

"No, boy! I forbid this sacrilege!" The old man's voice rose to a fevered pitch, his shouts strained and cracked into screams. "Dare you disobey the Lord's will? You are a weak-willed womanly boy!"

As if time had slowed down, in the warm amber glow of torch and lamplight mingling in the cool night air, Slocum saw a bullet pelt the earth just to the side of the boy. Screams and shouts of warning and panic arose from the little house. But the boy and mother continued walking toward each other, slowly, arms outstretched, some sort of shared joy writ large on their faces. Another bullet pocked closer, rooster-tailing dirt that spattered the boy, but still he kept walking, closing the gap between himself and his mama. Then he stiffened, both arms thrown to the heavens as if he had just found God and had to express himself in some meaningful way.

Then time became real again, and the boy lurched forward, a dark mass spreading as only blood can on the boy's dirty white shirtfront. He'd been shot square in the back. And the torch slipped from his hand and fell, harmless, to the dirt road. The boy dropped forward to his side, his head bounced against the hard-packed surface and his mother bent to him, scooped up his head into her lap, and cradled him. Slocum saw the boy, with one last effort, raise his arm and touch a limp hand to his mother's wrinkled face, then it dropped and Slocum knew the boy was dead.

Slocum was sure the old man's screams could be heard for miles. Soon, the old bearded bastard himself came stumbling down out of the rocks and staggered into the road, followed by his last remaining son, a hulking brute looking cowed and defeated.

"What . . . look what you made me do. Look, devils. I meant only to get him moving, get him to carry out the Lord's work. He was on a mission. But not this, not now . . . Oh, my boy, what have I done? What have I done?" He dropped to his knees on the other side of the boy, put his bald forehead to the boy's unmoving legs, and clutched at the thin, lifeless form as if it were a life raft on a roiling sea.

Soon the run-down house emptied and women and girls poured from it, clustering around the sad scene, weeping and holding one another.

Judith inhaled as if she would never again breathe normally, her thin body trembling with shock, grief, and anger. Slocum tried to crawl to her but she scrabbled to her feet and ran into the night, out behind the barn. He shouted once, but was sure she had not heard him above the din made by her weeping family. But she did not go to them. Soon, he heard hoofbeats rushing northwest into the night.

"Oh, Judith," said Slocum to the dark, empty space of the barn. "This isn't right. None of this should have happened."

He struggled to loosen his bindings, trying to gain himself enough slack to reach the knife in his boot. Soon, he heard fast footsteps running across the gravel yard, thick, thuggish steps, and his gut curdled at what that meant—the men, just the two of them, the old man and the older son, would soon find him. He was sure of it with each growl and grunt he heard. He wanted to at least meet them face to face, head on in a fight. They were cowardly backshooters, and he didn't doubt they wouldn't hesitate to kill him as he lay tied up, defenseless, helpless.

He thrashed and tipped over on his side on the musty old straw, the thin smells of rat shit and old, dried dung mingling with the thick dust in the air. He was trussed tight, his knees drawn up to his chest, hands lashed about the wrists and then wrapped around his legs. The sewn gash on his leg felt wet and throbbed tighter than Dick's hatband.

He almost bellowed to the women, the children, anyone, to look out, not to trust the men, but knew it was too late. The best thing he could do, he figured, was try to sit upright and push himself with his heels back into the dark corner behind him. If the men came poking about in here, with any luck they'd overlook him.

"Where's Judith?" The voice was that of the last young man just outside. Then Slocum heard a slap and a sharp gasp. Another slap. "Where is she? I asked you a question, Angel!"

He was hitting his sister? The very thought made Slocum sick. He'd never been able to understand nor stomach a man who hit a woman. That was the foulest of the foul, the lowest, and only rarely did a woman ever deserve such nasty treatment. There were viperous women in the world, to be sure, but they were the sort to claw out a man's eyes for his poke, then stab him when he was down. These women were not of that ilk. They were just caught between freedom and a Bible-thumper. One they wanted, the other they wanted to get away from.

But the thumper had spread his twisted madness to his boys, made them hate and regard the women as he did—as mere cattle for breeding purposes. And they were their own flesh and blood. Now look what it got them all. What a mad family. And yet, as he scooted backward into the corner, frantically working to grab hold of the hilt of his boot knife with his straining fingertips, he knew he couldn't let them down. He had to get free so that he might get them free.

Damn the old woman! If she hadn't tied him up, he'd be able to turn the tables on those bastards.

He wondered if she'd taken his rifle as well. Oddly she'd left him with his pistol. Just wanted to slow me down? he thought. Was that her game? Was she feeling so torn about the fact that her sons and daughters were getting killed and hurt? If the old man kept shooting, that's what would happen to them all, the children included. Maybe she was giving up. Giving in to the old Bible-thumper?

Shouts from the house alerted him to what was happening. He redoubled his effort, the throbbing of his leg wound be damned. He had to get loose, had to rescue Ruth, the twins, and Judith. There was no way he was going to let those God-fearing fools hurt those women. He had to get to them, get them free of those men somehow. Set them on their way to California. But first, Slocum, he told himself, you have to get that knife out of your boot.

He felt the hilt with his middle fingers' tips, but he was trussed so tight that there was little room for budging. He gritted his teeth, strained, felt the hemp tighten, heard it squeak and strain . . . and finally it budged a fraction more than it had. And now he wanted more and more. And by God, he told himself, he'd get that damn knife or he'd lose his hands trying.

Soon, he heard more noises, the deep cries of frightened children, interrupted by slaps that brought on harsher cries. Ruth's voice spoke sternly, but in a warm way to them, shushing them. He heard chains rattle, heard hard, stinging slaps against horses' rumps, and knew they were hooking up the wagon. The old woman's voice rose in pitch and was met with a smack and an oath from the old man: "Shut your mouth, woman! The Lord will not tolerate your wicked ways any longer! Your evil has resulted in killing on this night!"

Slocum gritted his teeth and resumed grasping for the blade. He hoped they didn't notice the Appaloosa. As if they'd read his mind, he heard one of the men speak.

"Where's that hired gun you got hid? Where's he at?"

Then Slocum heard a smacking sound and Ruth said, "He

isn't here! He was just a drifter, a low-down, dust-sucking scum who didn't want any part of this mess. He rode on as soon as the shooting got too intense."

He didn't know whether to laugh or be offended. He'd been called a pile of things in his years in and out of the saddle, but never a "dust-sucking scum." He supposed she had a right to be angry with him, but he figured she also knew he was trussed up in the barn.

They seemed to buy her story, because the man grunted and sounded as if he'd resumed working on the wagon. Slocum took advantage of the time to keep working on retrieving the knife. He was sweating and straining from his efforts, but his panting was covered up by the squeaks of the wagon wheels, the shouts of the men, the growling replies of Ruth and the twins, the occasional clipped cries of the children, and the distinct lack of sound from the mother and, more notably, Judith. And that gave Slocum pause. Had they caught Judith? Hurt her? Knocked her out perhaps? Or worse? And the old lady? He imagined she had just given up, convinced herself that she was doing the right thing in surrendering herself and her daughters to the foul whims of the beast men.

Soon, he heard the squeak and clomp of horses pulling a wagon. He heard the sounds of many feet receding, of random sobs, some children, some women. He imagined the deranged men, grim-faced, watching over their "herd" as they escorted them back to their farm for a life of drudgery.

It took him hours more to free a hand, then it was quick work to slice through the ropes that had caused his hands to purple and swell. As gray dawn light filtered in through the gaps in the barn boards and dawn slowly emerged, he risked leaning in the doorway of the barn to get a brief look at his leg wound. It throbbed like hell, but from what he could see, it wasn't infected—it didn't sport that swollen, angry red look that infected flesh wore. Despite his lack of care for it, the wound didn't appear any worse than it had the day before, and for that he was thankful.

It wouldn't take long for a wound like that to go so bad that he'd lose his leg. Still, he thought, a drizzle of whiskey on the sutured wound wouldn't hurt it. Now he only had to find his saddlebags, and soon. They turned up in the opposite corner of the barn he'd bedded down in. His saddle, blanket, and bridle and bit were by the saddlebags. And beside them, his rifle.

Now if only he could find the Appaloosa as easily. Slocum draped the bridle over his shoulder and hobbled on out to the paddock off the end of the barn. But there was no horse in sight. He hobbled farther, whistled, but still no horse. So, the sun-burned posse took the horse with them. But, he reasoned, Ruth's story about him would have been chewed to pieces when they did find the Appaloosa. Wouldn't they have come looking for him, and then surely would have found him trussed up in the barn? It's what he would have assumed, but then he wasn't them, a thug led by a half-assed preacher man—even if he was the remaining son's father.

He had to find Judith. He reasoned that she hadn't been found by them, or he would have heard otherwise, so she must be around somewhere. But there was no sign of the horse, nor of Judith. "Damn kid," he said, realizing that he couldn't leave, couldn't stay. The only thing he could do was back-trail to the Bible-thumper's farm, find his horse, and do what he could to save them. If they didn't want to leave, he had to get the heck out of there while he still had his life. Mueller, he owed that man a bullet, and Slocum vowed he would trail him to the ends of the earth for every wrong thing he'd ever done.

This entire interlude had been a long, costly one. His leg throbbed with every step he took. He searched throughout the house, the front, the back, around the barn, even for the body in the bushes. But there he found only blood on the ground and surrounding rocks. Maybe he didn't kill whoever it was. No, he'd been sure it had been a throat shot. They had probably lugged him off to bury at the farm.

He limped back to the barn and took stock of his situation. Everything the women had with them was gone, including their four horses, plus his horse, their possessions. The wagon, all of it. And the heavily laden wagon's wheels cut deep grooves back eastward, toward the farm where he'd saved the sunburned men.

"Should have left them to die," he muttered, rummaging

through his saddlebags. At least they hadn't found him, which in itself was curious. But if they did, he knew he'd be dead, bet on it. He had enough water in his canteen for a decent couple of reviving pulls, confident that he would be able to fill it at the little stream he'd passed on his way here—had it only been two days before?

He changed his shirt and checked his leg wound closely this time, looking for any telltale sign that an infection was developing. There was none, though he'd have a nasty welt once the wound healed. He stuffed the rest of his jerky and two remaining biscuits, now rock-hard, into his vest pocket; loaded his other pockets with spare ammunition; double-checked his Colt Navy, his knife, and his rifle; and headed eastward.

Once on the trail, and not knowing how many animals the men rode to get there, he had a tough time reading the tracks. He eventually determined that the main group didn't have his Appaloosa. But its shoes, different from the tracks made by the shoeless farm beasts, were there, though fresher and off to the side of the trail. It was almost as if whoever rode him was working hard to keep the tracks as unseen as possible. Probably, he nodded, because the rider knew he was going to follow. Which meant it couldn't have been one of the sunburned men, for they would have just killed him instead.

So who, then? Judith, of course. She was the one who had gone off on her own into the night, not wanting anyone else to see her. He'd assumed it had been her way of dealing with the shock and instant grief of seeing her brother murdered by their father. Luke had been closest to her in age, and had probably been her closest playmate. Slocum could only imagine how hollow and sad she felt inside.

Had she known the men were about to swoop in and clear out the place? Or perhaps she'd seen it happening and kept hidden—that seemed the likelier scenario to him.

She knew that Slocum had been trussed up in the barn, probably helped to do it. And then a thought stopped him in his slow, plodding tracks. The old woman and the coffee—it had seemed uncharacteristic of her at the time for a woman who'd just had one of her sons shot to bring the man who did it a cup of coffee. But the coffee itself tasted odd, he remembered. Bitter and harsh. He'd attributed it at the time to it being chicory blend or just plain burnt. It had been hot and that was all he really had cared about. Now, though, he wondered if she'd drugged him as she'd done to the sunburned men. Maybe Ruth had been in on it, too? Exercise him? Exhaust him further? Slocum's mind raced on, making connections where there were none.

He trudged on, trying to gain as much ground before the midday heat sapped more of his strength. Tracking them was simple, particularly because he knew precisely where they were headed. And he was relatively assured, too, that none of them were expecting him. Though he still kept alert and stuck to the roadside, ready to dive for what meager cover he could find should one of them decide to double back or lay in wait to ambush him.

In a way, Judith stealing his horse had saved his neck, which was what the women had partially intended. Kind of them, he smiled grimly. With friends like that . . . The men did buy Ruth's story about him leaving the day before. That meant Judith must have made off with the Appaloosa during the ambush, but had seen it happening, and then followed, hopefully at a safe distance. Relax, Slocum, he told himself. None of it really matters. At least not until you get there.

By his figuring, he had at least a couple of days' hard walking, in the best of health. But with this limp, he suspected he'd need another half day on top of that, at least. Unless he came across a miracle, like a stray horse. He chuckled, but try as he might, he couldn't see one in any direction. So he kept on walking.

The heat was brutal, and just about midday he headed for a rocky shelf that offered plenty of shade on the high side of the trail. Problem was, he wasn't the only one who thought so. A six-foot diamondback sensed his approach and did everything it needed to warn him off. Slocum sighed, out of striking distance. Since he didn't think he'd be able to jump back with his usual speed, he stayed well back of the beast while he considered what he was going to do next. He had certainly eaten his share of snake over the years. It reminded him of chicken, and while chicken wasn't his particular favorite meat, he preferred the hell out of it over starving.

The big boy was really rattling now. Slocum wanted that shady spot and the snake didn't want to give up his perch, so he had a decision to make. Walk on and leave the snake to its own devices? Risk a shot, for the meat and for his safety? Risk the clan hearing the shot and sending someone back to sniff around, see who was on their back trail? That was what he would do if he were in their position and heard a gunshot. But he knew they wouldn't do what he would. And even if they surprised him and did, he'd be well off the road and in a perfect spot to get the drop on whoever drew the short straw.

"Sorry, chum," said Slocum, "it's you or me." He cocked his rifle and, with a single shot, delivered the coiled and poised hissing rattler to his maker. A couple of short minutes later found him slicing the meat of the skinned snake into chunks. He didn't want any just now, but knew his body would need sustenance at the end of the day.

He dragged himself into the shade of the overhanging ledge and within a few minutes had slipped into a light slumber. He awoke sometime later—by the sun he reckoned he'd been asleep less than an hour, just enough to refresh him. He figured he could get a few more hours in before stopping for the night. He slid out of the ledge's shade and almost put a boot down right in front of another rattler. This one raised a fuss, and just as Slocum was ready to shoot it, the snake had the good sense to slither away, into the shade of a ground squirrel's hole. Slocum was relieved—he had no urge to waste another shot on a snake and he had a trail to follow.

Sometime later, a rabbit loped across the roadway in front of him. But he was lugging snake meat, and again, didn't fancy dealing with another carcass that day. He had hoped to make it to the little stream by nightfall, but well into dusk, he still hadn't reached it. He was tired and decided to keep on for a while longer. The moonlight, as it had been the previous two nights, was still strong, and the cooler air was welcome.

Soon, with a welcome relief that drew a deep-chested sigh from him, he heard the stream. Now he knew precisely how far he was from the farm. He also remembered a cluster of boulders just off the trail that had shown signs of scorching from a previous traveler's campfire, no doubt. He'd make a small fire, cook up his snake meat, drink his fill of water, and settle in for what he hoped was a decent night's rest.

And then, in the morning, he'd light off early and hopefully make it to the farm sometime in the late afternoon. If it was much later than that, he'd gauge his distance from it accordingly and wait out a few hours, then strike hard and fast in the middle of the night. Though he'd been mulling it over all day, he'd settled on no specific plan. And that was just the way it had to be—until he knew who and what he was dealing with.

But he could go in with a general sense of what needed doing. And first and foremost, he needed to get the Appaloosa and then, if it seemed like the decent thing to do, he'd assess whether butting his nose into the family's affairs any more than he had was even worth it.

But every time he decided to just grab his horse and go, he thought of those little kids, of the desperate looks on the women's faces, and knew their lives would be hell under the old Bible-thumper—worse than they had ever been, and judging from what he'd seen and heard, that was saying something.

He dumped the armload of tinder, kindling, and branches by the stones, toed a couple of them into place, and built a fire. He struck a lucifer with his thumbnail and set it to the slivers of bark, leaves, and a frayed snatch of cloth he'd sliced from his denims. They were ruined anyway and the cloth would make lighting the fire easier.

Within minutes, he had a decent little blaze cracking and snapping. The flames' light danced and wavered, bewitching his tired eyes. He shook his head and went back for that length of dried log he'd seen just out of the firelight, then scrounged up two more branches, thin whips ideal for spearing the meat he'd carried wrapped in the cloth sack where he'd also kept his biscuits.

In no time, the meat began to sizzle and drip, and he found himself licking his lips, in anticipation of eating. He wished he'd thought to bring salt, as that would draw out the flavor even more. "Beggars can't be choosers, Slocum, my boy," he said to no one but himself. It felt odd not to at least have the horse for company.

And as he dined, swearing to himself it was the best damned meat he'd ever had, he hunkered deeper into his vest and turned his thoughts to getting a plan formed. He wasn't quite sure just how to deal with the Bible-thumper and his band of acolytes.

He dragged the back of his hand cross his greasy lips and chuckled. Of course he would deal with them somehow. The men shot at him, shot at and grazed women, and didn't seem to care that there were children in the house. By all accounts they treated their women like cattle, mere breeding stock. Hell, Slocum had known ranchers who had more regard for their cattle, and who, while huge, solid men who brooked no lip or complaint from their hired hands, walked on tippy-toes around their wives and daughters, worshipping them and acting as if the sun rose and the moon set all for the women in their families. A far cry from the old crablike sunburned farmer.

What made a man so weak in the head that he succumbed to such savage behavior? It was one thing to believe in God, or any god, and the teachings in what so many called the "Good Book," but it was entirely another to allow it to stunt and warp your views so thoroughly that you treated anyone else as an inferior creature.

With these thoughts on his mind, Slocum, leaning back against the smooth rock, pulled his vest tighter around him. His leg, still sore, no longer throbbed, for which he was grateful. He slid his cross-draw holster with his Colt around so it sat snug against his satisfied stomach, and rested his fingertips on its use-worn ebony handle.

His rifle lay cocked and angled across his leg, and his hat angled low over his face, resting lightly on his nose tip. It smelled slightly of sunlight and dust and trails and wood smoke and sweat. The random cracks and snaps of the fire lulled him into a deep, hard, dreamless sleep.

The snapping and yelping of a dog awoke him sometime later. It was still dark and Slocum still felt tired, unrested, but there would be time for more rest later. Sounded like he had a coyote problem. He lay still, save for his eyes, which roved left and right, but he saw nothing. The little fire had dwindled down to a few glowing coals.

Keeping his back to the boulder, he laid tinder, then larger sticks, atop the coals. All the while the yelping and snarling continued, from far to his left, then to his right. That was how they worked, he knew. He'd had plenty of experience over the years with nighttime scavengers. And the worst part of it was that he wouldn't get much more sleep that night.

They must have sniffed the cooking snake meat. That smell could tempt most meat eaters for miles around. Couldn't really blame them. If he were hungry and afoot with no food and he smelled it, he'd probably invite himself to the campfire looking for a bite or two. He just had to make sure they didn't get a bite off his arms or legs. He'd had enough bleeding from wounds for a while, thank you.

They were brazen, though, and would most likely come at him in numbers, flashing their teeth and mangy hides, darting closer all the time to his fire. Hoping for a free meal. What they'd get would be a bullet in the head or chest.

And so his night went, several more hours of feeding the log he'd dragged over into the fire. Slocum had no intention of leaving the relative safety of the big rock he was leaning against. He kept the rifle cocked and positioned beside him, the Colt Navy at hand, and a big handful of bullets in his vest pocket. He'd found them easy to grab at times such as this.

The coyotes darted in and out again, their eyes reflecting and glowing like colored glass baubles in the firelight. He hoped Judith wasn't having such troubles. He hoped the log would last until morning, he hoped his leg wasn't becoming infected, he hoped the women were not suffering too badly under that tyrant, Rufus Tinker.

He hoped Tunk Mueller was at that very moment being strung

up by an irate rancher, just because he didn't like the looks of him. Slocum hoped a lot of things, and worked like hell to stay awake. But as gray light cracked the horizon, he lost the fight with sleep. His chin sagged to his chest as the last of the log reduced to cinders, and the yips of the damned coyotes trailed away toward some hidden den deep in the rocky countryside.

22

Slocum woke up in full daylight and cursed himself for wasting time and risking his hide with coyotes who would have liked nothing better than to sink their teeth into his leg or arm or head.

He spent a few minutes slowly unfolding himself from being huddled tight, trying to conserve heat. It had been a cold night, and since he'd had to travel light and fast, he'd left his gear hidden in the barn back at the little abandoned farm. And that meant no blanket or extra clothes. He stomped heat back into his good leg and massaged around the wound on his other leg to get his circulation flowing. No time for a campfire. Instead, he drank deeply from the canteen, then topped it off at the stream. The water made him cold, but he hit the trail and rubbed his arms on and off until the sun warmed him.

At mid-morning, he noticed a sudden lack of sound—no light bird chatter, no squirrels, even the breeze seemed to have dissipated. And then he heard a low, rasping sound, as if a fat man were walking along slowly, exhaling with each step he took. He'd been moving along at a decent pace, but had taken care to move as quietly as possible, not scuffing his boots on rocks, keeping to the softer spots, just in case the Bible-thumper or his son was prowling about. But now, with this new sound, Slocum slipped in among the trailside tree growth and boulders.

He crouched in silence, his rifle cocked, his pistol ready to be grabbed. The chuffing, sawing sound grew louder, closer, and then, across the trail and up a bit, he saw the massive honey-colored head of a grizzly. No wonder all the other animals had piped down. The thing looked to be a big male, small ears, shoulder hump wagging with each forceful step; the claws, curved surgical implements fully four inches long, wobbled with each step. The nose, almost as if it were a living creature all its own, roved left and right, sniffing for something to eat. This thing was death on four legs.

Slocum knew he was screwed. The beast, on all fours nearly chest height at the shoulder, would render him close to death with a single swipe from one of those forepaws. The creature looked to be in good health, and Slocum knew that shooting a rattlesnake was one thing, but a bull grizz? These things were born killers, instant to anger and, pound for pound, as tough as a wolverine but a whole lot bigger.

He'd have to get in a heart shot, then pray for a quick end. He considered shooting out the beast's eyes, but that would only make it angrier. And outrunning it wouldn't have been possible even if both his legs had been sound and in good shape, but he stood less than no chance of outrunning the grizzly with one pin ailing. No, his only chance was to sit tight, hope like hell the thing passed him by. He also wished he'd done some hunting on the trip and had more meat—a rabbit, anything that might satisfy this brute should it decide to sniff him out.

And then that's what it did. As it lumbered across the road, Slocum held his breath, kept perfectly still. He still had some broiled rattlesnake he'd been saving for later in the afternoon, but it looked like that time would not come. He heard his own heart thumping inside his head, felt his tongue and the inside of his mouth dry up as if he'd been dragging himself across the desert for days. Drops of sweat collected on his eyelashes. He didn't dare blink, so close did the creature seem. His eyes stung with sweat, with the urge to blink, drops clung to his nose tip, and crawled down his three-day beard, feeling for all the world as if he were a-swarm with lice.

He tried to calculate how long it would take him to open the cloth sack of snake meat swinging at his side. He figured he had about six pieces left. It was obvious the bear smelled food, and wanted it. That big black nose twitched and leapt side to side, up and down. The lower lip wobbled as the bear stepped ponderously forward, cautious and sniffing with each advance.

Slocum's hands grew tighter on his weapons, and he vowed to not go down without a fight. He also knew he might well be a goner, never again to know the warm, soft embrace of a woman, the clink of poker chips, the *punk!* of a cork popping out of a whiskey bottle, the bawl of cattle on a long drive, the singular sensation of riding the range alone . . .

And then the bear sniffed and grunted one last time, and padded down the road from the direction Slocum had come. He guessed it had already eaten recently. As he watched the great bear's backside waddle off westward, Slocum uttered a few words of thanks for whatever creature it was that had made a meal of itself for the bear.

He waited a good long time before he dared creep back to the roadway, then he hotfooted it toward his destination, despite the throbbing in his leg. The ache was just one more reason, he decided, to let those ungrateful men know exactly what he thought of them. It was a good couple of miles more before he slowed down on the neck swiveling as he checked his back trail for the grizzly. He knew from experience that they were wily trackers and would stop at nothing, distance be damned, to get at their prey.

Despite the bear episode, he saw by the height of the sun that he was making good time, and would be back at the farm by late afternoon. Just enough time to rest up, then hit them hard. A plan was slowly forming in his mind. He just needed the unwitting assistance of the sunburned men.

23

Just about the time he heard his stomach growl—he still hadn't tucked into the last of the snake meat, but had chewed two pieces of jerky—he smelled the light tang of wood smoke. Was someone else out traveling the road? It wasn't yet dark, too soon in the day for most travelers to make camp. Was it the Bible-thumper and his clan? Surely they would have made it back to their farm by now, unless they'd been forced to stop. Maybe the wagon had given out again. Slocum slowed his pace, checked his weapons, and advanced low, holding tight to the trailside shadows that grew longer with each minute as the sun descended to his back in the western sky.

Then he heard the throaty nicker of the Appaloosa. The horse had been with him long enough that he recognized the beast's sound. He was sure the horse was puzzled over this strange turn of events. It must be Judith, then, thought Slocum. And it occurred to him that she had taken neither his saddle nor his bridle. He'd seen her on the other mount the day before, and tough she did a serviceable job riding, she was no natural to the saddle. He reckoned she'd be sore by now.

And just off the road ahead, there stood Judith, standing with her backside bent toward the paltry flames of a small fire, rubbing her thighs and hips. He stepped into view, but it was the horse's nicker that gave him away.

Judith said, "Oh!" and spun to face him, clawing at her twin six-guns, but Slocum already had the drop on her. As she stared at him through the mask of anger, he thought he detected something else, relief maybe.

"No, no, no . . . horse thief. You leave those shooters right where they are, holstered and secure. Unbuckle that gun belt and toss it over here."

She did as he said, started to speak, and he cut her off. "I don't want to hear a damn thing, sister. I'll do the talking and I'll let you know when I want to hear from you."

Despite this, she said, "You won't shoot me. I saved your life."

"Oh, you did, did you? And by the way, I didn't give you permission to speak. Now back away from the fire and sit on that rock, hands on your knees." He snagged her gun belt and slung it over his shoulder. The horse stood hipshot tied to a tree a few feet away, so he went over and rubbed his neck. "Nice hackamore, Judith. Who taught you to do that?"

She scowled at him, then looked away, her eyes narrowed.

Slocum laughed. "Right, I forgot to give you permission to speak."

She turned back on him. "I don't need your permission to do anything!"

"Hush up a bit or we'll both be in the soup faster than you can say 'Holy Bible.' "

"Sorry. But we're still a couple of miles from the farm."

"I know. I was there, remember? I'm the one who—"

"Yeah," she said. "You're to blame for all this, you know. You're the one who cut them free."

"I prefer to think of it as saving their lives. Though I will admit having come to regret that decision. Not one of my shining moments, come to think on it."

She said nothing.

"Well, I'm glad to see there's some milk of human kindness in you." He sat by the little fire and stretched his legs out, careful to keep his Colt's grip angled to the front of his belt, in easy reach. He kept the rifle and her gun belt on the ground at his other side, well out of her reach.

Her stomach growled and she crossed her arms over her belly and looked at her feet. He saw her cheeks redden.

"You hungry, Judith?" he said, untying the sack from his belt. "You won't believe what I had to go through to get this—and then keep it." He tossed a chunk of the cooked meat in her lap.

She snatched it up and stuffed the entire thing in her mouth. After she'd chewed for a while, she said, her mouth half full, "It's good, what is it?"

"Finish it off, then I'll tell you."

She stopped chewing, stared at him, those green eyes narrowing again.

"You keep doing that, they're liable to stick that way. Then you'll go through life looking ticked off at every little thing."

"Maybe I am. And I asked you, what is this meat?" she said, chewing slower, the meat bunching in her cheek like a chaw of tobacco.

He finished his mouthful. "Snake."

She stopped chewing again, and her stomach growled. She swallowed the meat. "Can I have a drink from your canteen?"

He passed it to her. "So, are you going to tell me just what you're up to?"

"Why should I?"

"Because if you don't, I'll paddle you sore and drop you off at the doorstep of the farm. Though I'm sure that's nicer treatment than you'd get at the nearest town for horse theft."

"You wouldn't do that." But the statement rode up at the tail end, as if she wasn't so sure about him.

"Judith, I have about had enough of you, your family, this valley, the whole works. I want my horse, then I want to go away, far away from you all. None of you make any sense. Your mother wants to go to California, has wanted to for years, and when she finally gets up the nerve to leave that crack-minded father of yours, she encounters hard luck and buckles under to him again. I'm the only man who has probably ever been kind to you women and you tie me up, then steal my horse!"

Despite his order to her earlier to keep her voice down, Slocum found himself growling at her, his voice beginning to shout. He took another bite of snake, chewed, then leaned forward and said, "You give me one good reason why I shouldn't dump you with them and leave. One good reason."

She looked at her dusty boots again. "Because I love you."

"No," he said in a low voice. "No, Judith. You only think you do. You're too good for the likes of me, ma'am. You're special, you're young and full of the promise for the future. Besides, you're too young to be engaging in such acts. There's nothing wrong with them, mind you, but I'm an adult and so are your sisters. Don't be in such a hurry."

"Ruth said the same thing."

"Ruth's a wise woman. Look, the last thing you do if you care for someone is tie them up and steal their horse."

She looked at him with red-rimmed eyes. "We . . ." She looked down again. "I did it to save your life. I know what Papa's like, and . . . I was going to say 'the others,' but it's only Pap and Zeke left now, ain't it? But trust me, they would have killed you. Look what they did to Luke. Don't you see? You wouldn't have ridden away. Like I told you before, you're too good a person for that. You would have stayed and fought them, and they'd have killed you. So we did the only thing we could think of to save you. We knocked you out, then I had to figure out what to do with your horse. I hid. I was only going to tie it in the trees, but the men came storming in sooner than I expected. I wanted to help Mama and the others, but I froze. I couldn't think straight, not after they done that to Luke."

He rested a hand on her shoulder. She felt so thin and small. "You did the right thing, Judith. Don't worry." Then he lifted her chin and looked at her wet eyes. "You said 'we' before. Don't you think you should tell me the whole truth? If we're going to be working together, that is."

He handed her gun belt back without taking his eyes from hers. Finally she nodded. "Okay. It was Mama's idea. We all, well, she convinced us, after you shot Pete to protect me, and what with Ruth wounded, Mama was worried it would all end badly, with us all shot up. She said we could choose another time to fight, another time to leave. It would be harder in the future, but at least we'd be alive. Ruth and the twins were for it, and the children, well, they don't know their elbows from their behinds. They just want a sugar tit and a warm bed . . ."

Slocum smiled, nodded to encourage her.

"So, she somehow said she was going to send word to Papa and the boys that we were giving up. But Ruth and the twins and me . . ." She looked down again, picked at her dirty fingernails.

"So how did you knock me out? I don't recall taking a knock to the head."

"That was Mama. She put wolfsbane in that coffee she brung you."

He thought back, remembered its odd, bitter taste. "Isn't that some sort of poison?"

"Yeah, but she only used a little. It's an herb she dries. For medicines. You take too much, you can kill a body, but a little of it and you'll doze off for a good while."

"I know," he said, rubbing his neck. "I suppose I should be grateful I didn't wake up naked, tied to a fence."

She half smiled. "We all didn't want no harm to come to you. But we knew you'd get to scrappin' with Papa and the boys, and we were just sure they'd kill you and we didn't want that at all. It ain't your fight, Mr. Slocum."

He looked at her shining face a moment, then said, "I appreciate that, Judith. I really do, but I think you're selling me short. I have been known to hold my own in a scrap or two. But thanks just the same." He got up. "We better fetch more wood. I think we can risk a bigger fire. If what I know about your pa is true, he won't come at us until nightfall—if at all. He might be too busy . . ." He let the thought die there, wishing he'd kept his mouth shut.

"About as busy as you were with Ruth again, huh?"

He dropped his armload of wood by the fire and sighed. "Judith, I—"

She just winked and shook her head. "That's all right—she can't help it. Besides, Mama's right. Men are all the same. Even the good ones."

"Yeah, well, she may be correct in that assessment. I suppose it's true in my case, too. But you just wait a good long while before you verify it for yourself, you understand?"

Her smiled faded. "If they get me back there, I reckon I won't have that particular luxury."

Slocum's gut grew cold. He'd almost lost sight of the real reason for seeing that these women were freed from Papa Tinker's preachy grasp. He was a poisonous man who'd infected his own sons, and was working on a new generation of the same. He'd encountered such families in the past, but had done his best to steer clear of them. None of them had wanted to change their plight, but these women were different. Despite long years of abuse, the mother showed a strong backbone and had passed that to her daughters, too. But they needed help to make the final leap, help he knew now that only he could give.

24

"Well now, lookie here." Tunk Mueller toed then lifted the edge of the saddle with a worn boot, then bent and dragged it, the bridle and bit, and the saddlebags that had been laid atop it, out of the shadows of the run-down barn. He squatted before the gear, looking about the abandoned old homestead as he laid his rifle aside. "So, hell, that must have been Slocum after me. Recognize this as his fine gear from the Rockin' D. Sure glad I creased him. Now maybe it's time to find him and finish the job."

His horse, standing tied at the corral rail nearby, perked its ears at the sound of Mueller's voice.

Then he cackled, low and long. "And that means it was Slocum I shot. Thought I recognized his Appaloosa. And he's fetched up with them women, it seems. Yes, sir, this is a pretty picture, Tunk. Pretty as a newborn lamb." He gave the yard one more look, then unbuckled the saddlebags, riffling the contents and pausing as he unfolded a well-worn dodger. He stared at it a long minute, then ran a grimy hand across his week-old beard, scratching in concentration. He set it aside, riffled farther, and found a number of tasty items too good to pass up. Some of them were small and personal, by the looks of the care with which they'd been wrapped in cloth and squirreled in a buckskin pouch—a brooch, a pocket watch. There were papers, other useless items. But the brass spyglass could prove useful.

Mueller stood, cradling his rifle and walking slowly about the small yard between the barn and the house. Then he inspected the barn, found lengths of cut-up rope, a little bit of what he thought might be blood on the straw. Then he turned his attention back to the grounds, the hoofprints, bare footprints of children, boot prints of men, women. The house offered more of the same. He roved from spot to spot, making a mental accounting of all the activity that had taken place there, of the rough number of people involved.

As a man on the move these past few years, hounded by lapdogs and do-gooders, Mueller had developed a keen sense of caution. But even with all the sign about the place, he felt no familiar prickling up his spine and into his scalp, the usual way he knew without knowing when he was being tracked, stalked, or watched. Whatever had happened here, he concluded, had taken the participants elsewhere.

Mueller followed the tracks of the horses, the wheels from a heavy wagon, and lastly, laid over them all, the single line of boot prints leading in the same direction. "Slocum afoot," he said, his mouth spread wide, equal parts grin and sneer. "So that's what made you leave your traps behind." He bent low, tried to discern the age of the prints, sniffed at them, even wet a begrimed fingertip and dabbed it in the center of one sandy boot print. It tasted like grit and little else. He spat and rose. He'd never been much of a hand at tracking. But he could, by God, kill a man and rob him blind.

"No sir," he said, heading back to his horse and eyeing Slocum's saddle, bridle, and bags. He hefted the pile and lashed it on behind his own saddle. "Ain't no way I'm going to leave all this behind."

Mueller's thoughts turned to the grim scene he'd experienced but a day before out on the plain north of there. He still couldn't get that boy out of his head. All smiles, even as he was fixing to slice up strips off his mama's body to feed himself! And he'd offered some to Tunk, too. The gold teeth, now, they were something different. They were just going to waste. Precious metal, as the fancy folk called it, ain't got no business sitting pretty in a dead man's mouth. Might as well a living man enjoy it.

As he lashed the load onto the horse, he wondered what he might buy with the gold. A bottle or two, for starters. He lifted the neck of his shirt and wiped his mouth of sweat and chew juice. Maybe a new shirt, too. This red one might have been his favorite, but even a handsome garment comes to the end of its road. Hell, maybe I'll try a blue shirt next time.

The saddle and gear all sat nicely atop the dancing horse he'd borrowed for keeps from that belligerent Dez Monkton and his screaming biddy of a wife. All he'd wanted was a fair shake— and a look inside the man's safe. Had to have one, felt sure it must have been in the man's office. Hell, in his experience, every rancher worth his salt had at least a strongbox. If he had known that all he'd get out of it was a handful of silver tableware, he'd have skipped it altogether. Now he had Slocum dogging his back trail.

He smacked the jittery horse once on the flank. "Calm your worthless hide!" But it only served to have the opposite effect on the beast and it took him a full minute of yanking on the reins before the creature held still.

"Ain't no way I'm leaving this here outfit behind. I won't be back this way. After I kill me a Slocum, I'm going to keep on heading back, make sure them cooked farmers are for certain done for, then give their place a better look-see." He smiled at the memory of them. It had been his pleasure to leave them to die like that. Hell, it had even been amusing to see them try to look at him, all bubbled up and moaning, begging for water, for help. He sort of wished he had thought to do that to some- body. "Time enough yet," he told himself, with Slocum in mind.

"Bound to have something hid away in that farmhouse. I can find a secret cash hidey-hole better than any ten banditos, mark my words. Then I just may head northeast, circle wide. Make Canada by snow. Get me a squaw and hole up in a wig- wam or some such."

He cackled again and stuffed a knob of lint-covered plug tobacco, his last hunk, into his mouth. "Unless one of them wom- enfolk strikes my fancy. I do wonder what they are doing heading eastward. But hell, they're women. Who can know what's in such a creature's mind?"

The horse walked on. It didn't matter to Mueller that he was talking only to his horse. It was company enough. He'd never really gotten on with other people, but horses never complained nor said he was talking too much. "I avoided them when I come through here because they was all totin' guns and I don't fancy getting shot up by a woman. They're liable to shoot off parts of me I'm partial to." He patted the mare roughly on the neck. "You wouldn't know about such things, I know, but not ol' Tunk."

He laughed and worked the chew in earnest, avoiding the back teeth on the right side, tender ever since that fistfight with a couple of uppity hands at the Rocking D a month or more before. A fight he'd been enjoying when that damned Slocum had stepped in, settled his hash, and called an end to the fight.

Mueller sent a stream of brown chew juice tailing into the dirt, missing the spiderweb for which he'd aimed. "Lousy do-gooder." He glanced again at the found gear. "I am owed that much and more by that foul bastard, just for putting up with his meddling. By God, I'll settle *his* hash this time. Wounded and afoot, he'll be near useless."

The horse nickered. Mueller took that to mean the horse agreed with him, so they headed down the lane, eastward toward that farm. The second saddle, tied on poorly, flopped against the dun's rump, keeping her agitated, but if Tunk Mueller sensed it, he didn't act on it, so engrossed was he in his one-sided conversation. Soon he lapsed into chatter about the viciousness of his dead mother and his father's inability to get his head out of the demon bottle.

Then his thoughts turned to the nest of gamblers and whores he'd discovered just over the border in Ojinaga the previous summer. What a fine old time they had had—until he'd lost and lost, one hand after another, at the tables, and had been forced to shoot his way out of that town. It hadn't been the first time he'd killed a woman, but the first time he'd killed one he'd grown to like. He couldn't recall her name, but she had been a saucy thing always read for a romp.

Soon enough, he fell silent, knowing that since he was so

poor at reading sign, he might at any time catch up with Slocum, and it wouldn't do to have the man hear him before he could get the drop on him. All he needed was one clear shot, from the side, rear, front, didn't matter. Only thing he wanted to do was kill Slocum. The rest could maybe identify him, but Slocum for certain could. And that was why that nosy do-gooder was going to die.

25

Slocum checked his rifle and said, "Where does your mother keep that wolfsbane?"

"They'll never let you get close enough to put it in their drinks. Not after what we did to them last time."

He smiled. "Who said anything about putting it in their drinks? You let me worry about getting close enough and I'll get it into their mouths, no worries there." They have mouths, thought Slocum, and I have fists to jam into them, gun barrels to jam down them. They'll eat the damned leaves . . . even if it kills them. "First things first, we have to figure out the finer points of rescuing your mother and sisters."

"What if they don't want to be rescued? Seems to me they went of their own mind," she said.

"Maybe so, maybe not. From everything I've heard, they'll still be waiting for the right time to do it. And judging from what I heard the old man saying, it'll be a cold day in hell before he lets them out of his sight. So it's up to us to make it happen. You ready?"

She nodded, frowning at him.

"And wipe that scowl off your face, girl. I told you before, you're too pretty to go around looking angry all the time. Your

149

face will stick that way and then where will you be?" Then he winked at her.

"Okay, Mr. Slocum, so what's the plan?"

"How many shells do you have for those six-shooters of yours?"

She felt the gun belt, fingering each filled bullet loop. "Seven on the belt and five in each gun."

"None under the hammer, right?"

"Course not. I might look young, but I ain't stupid."

"Never said you were—just a mite sensitive."

"I'm also going to need to know where that arsenal of theirs is. Your mother said something about it being in the barn. Is that true?"

"Yeah, but it's locked tighter than a bull's backside. You won't be able to get in there without a key or explosives."

He wagged his eyebrows and nodded.

"You got dynamite?"

"Nope," he said, "but I do have gunpowder, as a last resort. How many keys do you think there are?"

She scrunched her eyes, "Oh, I bet there's only one. Papa don't trust no one. I thought he kept a key on a leather thong around his neck, but Mama couldn't find it before we left. Then we just ran out of time, had to get moving."

"Well, I'll cross that bridge when we get to it. If we're going to pull off whatever sort of plan we can come up with, we need to work together. You have to do what I say and no questions, you hear me?"

She took longer than he would have liked to answer him but she eventually nodded.

"Good. First thing I want to do is get him and your brother, Zeke, out of the house, and subdue them."

"What's that mean?"

"It means I knock them on the head, then we both drag them off and tie them up. By my own count there are only the two left." He felt bad bringing up the fact that three of her brothers had died within the last day, but if it bothered her, Judith didn't show it.

She nodded her head. "It'll be a blessing to have them quiet for a spell, especially Zeke, on account of him being so foul-mouthed and all. Even Pap doesn't like him to talk too much. I reckon that's what they call poetic justice."

Slocum just stared at her, unsure what exactly she was talking about.

"Oh, you know, Pap's big on that sort of thing. Said it's all in the Bible. I haven't spent a whole lot of time with the Bible, as I'm a girl and Pap says that girls don't have any right to know any book learning. But Mama taught us each how to read and do our figures. She said it would be useful someday."

"Sounds to me like Ruth isn't the only clever one in the family."

She nodded. "Mama's right smart."

"I don't want them to know how many of us there are, so we'll keep hidden. I'll use you as bait, then see if we can lure them out that way."

"You'll use me as . . . bait? I look like a worm to you, Mr. Slocum?"

He heard her, but was already on the move, taking stock of their meager possessions. They had his sheath knife, boot knife, three pistols, and a rifle, plus his Appaloosa.

"We'll have to leave the horse here," he said. "For now. We're going on a scouting mission. We can't risk the other horses sensing him, making a fuss." Normally, he wouldn't leave the horse anywhere else, but he did have to move in on the little fortified compound and quick. He retied the horse, then motioned for her to follow him. "Double-check to make sure those are loaded and ready, just in case," he said, indicating her pistols.

"In case of what?"

"In case someone sees us." He looked at her. "No offense, Judith, but I don't trust any of them as far as I can throw them."

She laughed, "You and me both."

It took them most of an hour, but by the time they came to the farm, Slocum noted that he still had a few hours before dark. They'd traveled on the lane until they drew close, then broke right and climbed the rocky knob directly across from the farm.

"Up here," Judith whispered. "It's a good spot for spying on 'em. I come up here sometimes to get away from them all." They lay on their bellies behind a bristling row of scrub brush.

"Where's the outhouse?" he whispered, eyeing the house. All this would be so much easier if he could just shoot the men. It would solve a lot of problems. It might not be quite the right thing to do, but then again, was what they were subjecting the women to right?

"Straight out back from the kitchen. Two-seater."

"How far?"

She paused. "Far enough. You gotta go?"

"No." He stifled a laugh. "Is there a time, more than others, when your father does his business?"

"Yeah, Pap's regular as a wound watch. Mornings, just after breakfast, before daylight."

"He eats early."

"Yep, all the men do." She grew silent a moment, thinking, no doubt, about her dead brothers. Then, in a whisper, she said, "Women aren't allowed to eat with the men, can only eat when the men have gone outside. And if Pap comes back in and finds them, he gets riled and commences to throw dishes, upends the table. Claims women shouldn't be seen to be eating, claims it's a sight no one should see."

Slocum leaned out a little beyond the bushes rimming their perch and looked toward the barn. He had to admit, for a crazy person, the old man kept a neat place. Everything looked tidy; even the wagon Slocum had mended was parked next to a two-seat buggy and a hay rake and a plow. He kept looking around the buildings, looking for a way in, something that might help spring the women without forcing a gunfight. But he saw nothing.

"I'm going to head down to the barn while I still have daylight, see if I can uncover the old man's stash of weapons, anything else I might find of use."

"How are you going to carry them?"

"I'm not. I'll hide them on him, take what I need. Now where in the barn is it?"

Judith didn't respond.

"Judith, where is his hiding place?"

"I don't know. It was Mama and Ruth who found it. I was busy . . . tying up the men." She looked down at her lap. "Me and the twins. Then Mama and Ruth come back and helped us. Then we had to leave."

"Okay then. I'll go down and scout around, then come back here. If I get cornered, you stay put. I don't want to have to rescue you, too. I'll need you once I settle on a final plan. Some of it depends on what I find in the barn."

He rose, crouching low, then looked back at her. "I'm serious, Judith. You keep my rifle handy and stay put. Promise me?"

She nodded. "But what if Papa or Zeke should head to the barn? I could make a noise, hoot like an owl."

"Good point." He paused. "But it's too risky. If you were to whistle, something like that, you'd be found out. Best leave it to me. I've had practice at this sort of thing." He smiled at her and patted her shoulder.

She placed a hand up quickly atop his, brushed her cheek against his hand. "Please be careful."

He carefully slipped his fingers free. "Yes, ma'am." He smiled again and made his way down the far side of the hill. That kid, he thought, she's falling for me and that's a dangerous game. But he pushed that worry from his mind as he made his way from boulder to boulder, aware that he could be seen from the house for part of his journey from the lane to the barn. But there was no way around it.

He needed the daylight to snoop around in the barn, and from what the women said, there was something of value in the barn that the old man kept hidden, something that they guessed was probably a store of weapons and ammunition. Though for what reason he would have such things, Slocum was unsure. At the moment, he didn't really care. He just needed to find it and get the men out of there, then figure out some way of getting the women and kids away and free.

He made it across the road and dropped into the tall hay in

the corner of the field separating him from the barn. The waist-high grasses were a golden swaying mass under the heat of the midsummer sun. He moved slowly but steadily, lest anyone see the grass moving, grow curious, and come to investigate.

He made it to the edge of the field near the front doors of the barn, and was about to crawl onward so that he would be even with the backside of the barn. From his brief visit days before, he recalled seeing a smaller door there. He could pry it open if it was locked from the inside. Slocum resumed belly-crawling when the front door of the barn opened and out stepped Zeke. He closed and bolted the door behind himself, then headed to the house.

Slocum took a good look at him. His skin tone had improved slightly since they'd first met, though he noticed the man was still wearing loose-fitting clothes and walked with his arms slightly raised and his legs apart. Slocum couldn't help smiling—there was a man who was chafing from sunburn.

He wouldn't have locked anyone in there, reasoned Slocum, so the barn must be empty. He waited until the man made it to the house, then continued wriggling through the grass, pulling himself along on his elbows, his wounded leg now throbbing each time he set his knee to move forward.

Finally, he made it even with the back of the barn and, rising to his feet, ran hunched over, crossing the twenty or so feet until he made it behind the weathered structure. He leaned there, paused, controlling his breathing, listening for shouts or the rush of boots crossing the hard-packed yard, but heard none. Good. Keeping his back to the weathered boards, he edged along the back of the building until he came to the small door he remembered had been there. He drew his Colt and raised his other hand above his head and tried the edge of the door—and it swung open. No sound came from inside, no gunshots, no cocking of guns, nothing. He peered around the door frame, peeked into the darkened interior, then keeping low, he dashed through and softly closed the door behind him.

Once inside, Slocum stepped to the side, away from the door, and let his eyes adjust to the darker light of the barn. If I was the old Bible-thumping madman, where would I hide a stash of weapons or anything, for that matter? The stable floor was typical of its ilk, packed dirt, save for the very center directly before the great double doors. It was planked with long-worn boards, corduroy fashion so that heavily laden wagons might not sink into the floor. Though here, with such hard, dry ground, this would seem to be an unnecessary precaution.

Slocum walked over to the boards, careful to stay to the side lest the sound of his boots on the boards give him away to anyone who might be outside. He bent low and ran a hand over the worn planks, hoping to detect any that might have been disturbed recently. But the hay chaff on them, and dirt to the side, all seemed untouched. That was curious.

He rose and eyed the boards from another angle. But knowing he really didn't have time to kill in such speculation, he turned his attention to the stalls lining the side of the barn. Then he heard footsteps approaching the front door.

Without a second glance, Slocum worked his way up the straight wooden ladder as fast as he could to the hay loft, just as whoever had entered the barn shut the door behind them. Slocum paused but a few feet from the top of the ladder, crouched low. Whoever had come in had also paused.

Slocum wondered if they had seen him, then got his answer. "Who's there?" came a woman's voice, just louder than a whisper. "I saw hay falling. I know somebody's up there." Boots sounded on the board, moved closer to the bottom of the ladder. "Judith, honey, is that you?"

Slocum recognized it as the voice of one of the twins. She was probably safe to confide in, but he didn't know for certain just where her loyalties lay now that they'd elected to come back to the farm. He decided to wait, hoping she'd climb up. If she headed toward the door again, he'd have to stop her, or risk having her spill the beans about an intruder in some misguided attempt to appease her father.

He heard her boots on the ladder and stayed put, waiting in the shadows. "I'm coming up, whoever you are." Her voice drew closer, then her head and shoulders appeared above the top of the ladder. "Mr. Slocum!"

"Shhh!" he said, tapping an extended finger to his lips.

"Come up here, I need your help." She smiled and hurried up the ladder and into the loft.

"What are you doing here, Mr. Slocum? Is Judith with you? We're worried sick about her."

"Judith is fine, but I need your help." He squinted at her. "Can I trust you?"

She walked toward him on her knees, and with her face inches from his, she nodded. "I'll prove it to you." And before he could answer, she hiked up her dress and straddled him, her hands on his chest.

"Mary or Angel, I don't know which you are, but I don't have time—"

She closed her mouth over his, then pulled back enough to murmur, "I am Mary, and there's always time for this."

And despite his earlier sense of urgency, Slocum found himself sinking back into the soft hay with this luscious woman atop him. He tasted her sweet breath and wanted more, the heady scent of her clouded his senses, filling his nose and lungs. She unbuttoned the front of her dress and peeled it apart to reveal her curvy, naked body before him. With each passing second, he found himself filled with the increasing urgency of lust. Soon, he, too, was partially unclothed. He flipped her over so that he knelt over her. He worked his way up the taut, heaving plane of her belly, trailing the tip of his tongue along smooth flesh grown hot to the touch.

Mary's hands, on either side of Slocum's head, guided him upward as much as her low, impatient moans. He paused at her perfect, full breasts, the nipples, firm as raspberries not yet ripe, glowed scarlet in the near-dark of the loft.

By the time his lips reached her jutting, trembling chin, her mouth sought his, frantic and frenzied. Their teeth tapped together. Slocum tasted something bitter on his bottom lip, and didn't care. This woman could draw his blood all day long and he felt sure he could take it. Keeping up with her was another problem, though. With one strong farm girl's hand she kneaded his backside, drawing him in tight between her wide-spread legs, with the other she groped between their straining bodies slicked with a sheen of sweat, for the length of his firm member.

She proved more than ready for him, and before he realized it, Slocum had slipped into her. She gripped his bottom lip gently with her own and a soft, humming sound, as if from a swarm of approaching bees, rose from her throat, her nostrils working to keep up with her hot breath pushing in and out, keeping time with his increasing thrusts.

In a deft move Slocum didn't sense coming, Mary grasped his shoulders, shifted her weight hard and fast to her left, and rising up onto one knee, rolled Slocum once more onto his back. She glanced down once at him, grunted, and smiled as she pushed his shoulders flat to the soft hay, her cotton dress, unbuttoned up the front, parted wide and slipped down her slender upper arms. She arched her back, pushing her full breasts outward. They bounced and wagged with each energetic slide downward she made, their bodies where they connected slapping together. Slocum grasped them, firmly massaging her breasts against her taut frame.

Then she rose up, nearly lifting him with her, before slamming downward again. Her eyes remained closed, but the lashes fluttered as if she were in a deep sleep, dreaming of something. Pleasurable or frightening? wondered Slocum.

Her braid had worked loose and thick hair the color of dark, polished leather hung to either side of her face. Sweat-soaked strands lay plastered to her cheeks, across her chin, and her mouth pulled wide in an almost-smile, her full red lips seeming to tremble in anticipation. Her hands gripped and rubbed and kneaded his ribs. He was nearly there, despite himself. There was something about this girl that made him—

"You 'bout done up there, Mary?"

Slocum's breath stopped fast in his throat. In a single move, he rose to his elbows and stared at the girl, her face inches from his. And she was smiling, it looked to him, at his reaction. So she wasn't surprised by the familiar-sounding voice below them in the barn.

"It's only Angel," said the girl, giggling loud enough for their unexpected visitor to hear.

"And who else?" hissed Slocum, his eyes wide, his breath not yet come back to him.

She giggled again. "Surely you remember my twin sister."
Mary watched him a moment, suddenly unsure of his reaction.

Slocum squinted at her in the near-dark barn, and sighed.
"Tell Angel she'll catch cold standing down there."

"Angel . . . oh, there you are."

Slocum looked toward the ladder in time to see the twin of
the girl straddling him rise into view. Other than Mary's wild
hair filled with chaff—and her lack of clothing—Angel and
Mary appeared identical, indeed. As Angel crawled toward him
on her hands and knees, a familiar grin on her face, Slocum
wondered just how identical they were.

A short while later, though they had worked him mercilessly,
Slocum felt oddly rejuvenated.

"That was nice, Mr. Slocum," Angel said. "Don't you think
so, Mary?"

The other girl nodded. "Nothin' finer. Now, just what were
you doing in the barn, Mr. Slocum?"

"What I came looking for and what I found are two different things. I wonder if you two ladies might be able to tell me
where your pap keeps his secret stash, the one that's all
locked up?"

"Oh, that," said Mary, finishing up her buttoning. "I'm not
sure."

"Me either," said Angel. "But I expect Ruth and Mama know.
We was busy out front that day we left, trussin' up Pap and the
others to the fence."

Slocum nodded, recalling that Judith had said the same thing
to him. "Okay, I better get going. I'm working on a plan to get
you all out of here. But I'm going to need some help."

"Okay," they both said at the same time.

"Before dawn, I'll need you two, and Ruth, your mother,
and the kids all to get in one room and keep low."

"That'll be easy. Papa locks up all us women together at
night anyway," said Mary.

For once, the old man's foul ways might work in Slocum's
favor. He nodded and began down the ladder, then stopped and
looked over at them as they helped each other pick hay chaff
from their hair. "It's been a most instructive time, ladies. And

I thank you. Until later." He touched his hat brim and smiled at them.

They giggled as he disappeared down the ladder. Slocum didn't quite know what to think of what had just happened, but he knew he'd better put it out of his mind and come up with a solid plan, and fast.

26

Despite his vow to himself that he would stay awake and alert, keep an eye on the tracks, the heat of the day, the slow plodding pace of the horse, and the lack of sleep he'd had over the past long week wore on Tunk Mueller. Soon his eyelids lost the struggle and closed, the rhythmic motion of the tired, underfed horse mimicking what Mueller had always imagined a ride in a boat might be like. Though he had vowed he'd never climb into such a thing. Hell, he was no fish. He even avoided crossing rivers that required the horse to swim, which in turn would necessitate his getting dunked. How could those cowboys on trail drives shuck off and carry their goods on their heads as if they were ducks, grabbing hold of a saddle horn or stirrup and following their horses?

No, sir, and thank you, ma'am. Water was a thing he avoided at all costs. He even preferred the liquids he took in to be of a medicinal nature, if at all possible. He sure hoped the farmhouse with those sunburnt farmers decorating the fence out front would have sufficient libation inside. Else he might have to shoot the dead men out of spite. And they would deserve it, too.

His horse's nickering startled Mueller into wakefulness. He sat up from his slumped position and opened his eyes wide, careful to look around, see if he'd been watched. But he saw no one. Then he heard a horse again, off to his right. But it wasn't his horse.

He slipped from the saddle, sliding his rifle from the boot, and bent his head below the beast's withers. He waited a long minute, watching his horse's ears and the direction it looked. He heard no other sound as he eased around the front of his hose, kept the reins in one hand, his rifle in the other. He didn't dare cock it, but knew he should. He'd drop to the dirt and cock it as he rolled, that's what he'd do should someone take aim from the trees where the horse sound came.

A rustling from behind the low trees paused Mueller. He poked the barrel of his rifle into the leafed branches and parted them, leaning to one side. It revealed a clearing, and in the midst of it, there stood a horse staring at him with ears perked forward. Mueller peered closer, saw that the horse was unsaddled, but tied and rope hobbled. He saw no one about the spot, so he whispered, "Hey! Hey over there!" No one responded.

He parted the bushes farther. It was Slocum's horse! The Appaloosa. What sort of game was Slocum playing at? Leave his saddle and things back at the barn and then leave his horse here, tied in the bushes? But wait, Slocum had left the old abandoned farmstead on foot. So what was his horse doing here? Unless it was a trap. None of this made any sense to Tunk, but he figured, nasty as she was, his mama didn't raise a fool.

He kept low and got on the far side of his horse again, kept it between him and the direction the other horse stood, and eased his horse back down the road a piece. This required thought. And the more he stood there, gun cocked now and ready to kill, the more confused he became.

What in the world could this mean? Couldn't be that there was no one around. After all, who would leave a perfectly sound horse unattended? Then a smile came to his face. What if his shot had been a better one than he thought and Slocum had died somewhere along the way? Crawled off and just died? It was a bittersweet notion, to be sure, but one that Mueller figured he could live with. He'd be denied staring at the man as he wet himself and took a few rounds to the head, but then again it would be one less chore for him to put up with.

Then he shook his head as if to dispel a bothersome fly. No, no, that wouldn't explain the horse being here, because Slocum was on foot when he left that old place. So someone took his horse, left him afoot, and now what? "Aw, hell," he said and tied his horse to a stunted pine. Before he could change his mind, Mueller strode straight into the clearing, his pistol drawn, his rifle aimed and waist high.

The Appaloosa whickered nervously, stamped a foreleg, and spun to keep Mueller in sight.

"Easy, damn you," he said, low and growly, swiveling his head side to side, then turning in a circle, guns at the ready. But no one attacked, no one shot, no one did anything, because, he soon realized with a grin, there was no one around. His smile slid a bit. Didn't mean there wouldn't be someone around soon, though.

A few yards away sat a blackened fire ring. He walked to it and bent, looking around for surprises, and rested a hand on the coals. Long cold. He stirred them with a finger, not even warm. "Hmm," he grunted.

His own horse neighed and Mueller peeked out from between bushes, but the horse was alone, looking his way. Okay, then the horse was alone, left here for some purpose he didn't know of, and he didn't really care. It was his horse now.

He holstered his pistol, slid out his sheath knife, and with care, and keeping an eye on the Appaloosa's mouth, slashed apart the hobble. The rope separated and part of it fell to the ground. As he led the horse out to the road, the other half slipped off the horse's leg.

He kept up his vigilance, just in case he was being watched, but by the time he got the Appaloosa alongside his horse, and the two busied themselves with the strange behavior they had of greeting each other and sizing up the other, he felt sure he was alone. But that didn't mean someone wouldn't be back for the beast. The fact that it was Slocum's was just too good a deal to pass up. Not that he wouldn't have taken it anyway. A horse is a horse and surely someone would pay handsomely for a solid beast such as this.

He managed to get it saddled and bridled without too much

trouble, then he tied the reins together and led it along behind. All the while his glance rabbited left to right with each sound, real or imagined. It was a couple of miles before he began to relax. And as the first signs of dark came on, he felt pretty comfortable with the notion that John "Do-Gooder" Slocum's Appaloosa and gear were his to keep. Now he just had to find the man himself and do away with him.

Just when he began giving thought to making camp for the night, then hitting the farm early in the morning, he recognized features of the landscape, most notably that knob of rock up ahead to his right. That would be the high rocks directly across from the farm, he remembered that much. He urged the horses into a trot, and within minutes, just as the light was fading, he saw the distinct outlines of the fence, the house, and beyond it, the barn. All neat and tidy. But something was wrong . . . he slowed his pace.

There was lamplight in the windows. He rode closer, though slower and quieter, lest whoever it was got wind of him. And he got his second shock—there were no dead men strapped to the fence out front. Not even a sign of them.

"Hmm," he grunted, and righted his horse before the front gate. Could be Slocum in the house. Could be them women, he had no idea at this point, but one thing was certain—it damn sure wasn't them sunburnt men. They'd be dead for sure. But it would be just like Slocum to bury their damn farmers' hides.

No time like now, Tunk Mueller told himself, and levered a round in his rifle.

27

Slocum had made it to the top of the rocky knoll overlooking the farm and found Judith waiting for him. But her attitude was cold, and she appraised him with slitted eyes. He had been back for twenty minutes, and had told her what he found—or didn't find—though he eliminated the twins from his report. Finally, just as darkness began to drive the sun westward, Judith spoke. Her voice was cold, distant.

"Mr. Slocum."

"Yes, Judith." He turned his attention from watching the house back to her.

"I saw the twins go into the barn."

Here we go again, he thought. "Look, Judith, we've been over this. I am an adult—"

"And I am not a child!"

"Keep your voice down," he whispered. "And I never said you were."

At the same time, movement along the road, far to his left, caught his eye. Something was moving their way, from the direction they had come earlier. As it recurred, then drew closer, he groaned.

"What's the matter?" said Judith.

He wished he had brought the horse. And his collapsible spyglass. "You remember that man I was trailing?"

"That Tunkey fella?"

"Yeah," he said. "Tunk Mueller. Well, he's back. And from the looks of it, he has my gear and my horse."

Judith wriggled closer to the edge and peered down. "Oh, hell no."

"Now, Judith!" whispered Slocum, then caught himself. "Sorry. I suppose that sounded like your father . . ."

"Not hardly, Mr. Slocum. If I swore in front of him, he'd hit me."

She kept looking at the house, and said it with such simplicity that he was surprised for a moment. The feelings of guilt and anger roused in him and he vowed again to get these women out of the clutches of the misguided, Bible-howling crazy man. But first, he had to deal with the killer. What in the hell was he doing here?

Maybe I'm seeing things, thought Slocum. He rubbed his eyes with his knuckles and looked again. Yep, it was him. That Tunk Mueller was audacious, he'd give him that. He hated the fact that this murderer had found his gear and now was just sauntering on in with it all. It had been a long time since he'd felt so frustrated. "At least I have my guns."

"And me." Judith sneered down toward the red shirt just visible in the dwindling light of dusk. The steady *clop-clop* of both his horse and the Appaloosa's hooves on the hard-packed trail continued for a few more paces, then came to a stop in front of the farm gate.

Mueller sat there a moment, then shouted, "Hello the house!"

Within seconds, the front door swung wide. Warm light spilled out and illuminated the outline of big, shaggy Zeke holding aloft a lantern. "Who's there and what do you want?"

The man on the horse took his time in responding. Finally, he said, "Wondered if you've seen a stranger around these parts?"

"Just you, mister. Now as I asked before, what do you want?"

"No need to get your hair in a knot. I'm tracking a man, a

known killer. I wounded him a few days back and now he's afoot. I got his horse here, his gear, too."

The man stepped down off the porch, and another large dark shape emerged onto the porch, carrying a long gun. The first man approached the mounted man, a shotgun held poised in one big hand, the lantern in the other. He drew close, held the lantern high, and inspected the horse. "Where'd you get this horse?"

"I recall telling you that not but a few seconds ago."

"Don't get smart with me. I didn't come sniffing around here, you did. Now where'd you get the horse? If you're looking for the man, seems to me he'd be near his horse."

"Good thinking, there, farm boy. But the funny thing is, I found it just up the road a piece. And funny thing, his boot prints were there—and so were smaller prints, like maybe them of a woman. You got any notion who that might be and why they'd be so close without you all knowing?" He snorted and shook his head, as if he knew something they didn't.

The man lowered the lantern and headed back to the house at a fast walk. "Pap!" he said as he walked.

A voice from the porch said, "What? Who's he? What's he want?"

Before the man with the lantern could answer, the man a-horseback said, loud and sounding frustrated, "I am a traveler looking for information and, if I may be so bold, a place in your barn to sleep for the night. That's it, that's all. If you can't accommodate me, I guess I'll move on down the lane."

"Now hold on there, stranger," said the second man, who Slocum knew to be the old man. He stepped down from the porch. "Ain't nobody said you had to leave. We got room in the barn, got food on the table. Follow Zeke here to the barn. He will see to your horses, then you come on in and we'll see if we can each provide answers the other man's looking for—over a good, hot meal. Eh? How's that suit you?"

"Right down to the ground, sir." Mueller urged his horse forward, walking it to the barn, the Appaloosa following.

Slocum smiled. Mueller had saved him a trip back to the

old ruined farm where he'd met the women. He'd also saved Slocum from having to trail him, provided he could get the drop on Mueller before the outlaw killed him.

"Mr. Slocum," whispered Judith. "Papa's up to something. Only time I ever heard him talk that nice is when he's about to let Mama into his bed. And I ain't never heard him say anything that nice to a stranger. What are we going to do?"

"We're going to capture the lot of them."

"How?"

"I'm working on that." He was glad it was darker now, so she couldn't easily tell by his creased brow that he had no plan. Mueller's arrival had skewed everything—but it just might work to their advantage.

"Fat lot of good sittin' up here's gonna do us," she said. "Might as well just walk on down there and give ourselves up." Judith scowled, and finally looked at him. "Hey, what are you smiling about?"

"I'm smiling," he said, still trying to keep his voice lowered, "because you're some smart, for a kid, you know that?"

"What's that supposed to mean?" Her scowl was gone, but she wasn't sure what to think.

"Don't worry your pretty little head about it. I have a feeling you're tired. And I know I am. I've been lugging my injured leg around all day long, and I'm tuckered out."

"Well, let's go back to our campsite then."

"What would the point of that be, Judith?" he said, barely able to see her as the light faded. "Nothing there once we get there. Mueller got my horse, in case you didn't notice. And that's the only thing we left at your campsite—other than a fire ring."

"We could . . ." She cast her eyes downward again. "Yeah, you're right. So we just stay here?"

Slocum rolled over. "You have a better idea? I think it's just about ideal, what with our perfect view of the farm—I can see why you chose the spot as a hiding place—and we can track the comings and goings. Now, if I'm going to walk on in there later, I'll need some rest. I can barely keep my eyelids open. You take first watch. Wake me in a couple of hours."

"Hey," she said. "What about me?"

But he was already half asleep. And soon, he was all the way there.

28

After a too-friendly supper, by the time Mueller got back to the barn, he was sure of a few things. The old man had to have money hid in the house somewhere. Place was too nice not to have some sort of cash box. He'd missed out on it at the Rocking D, but he would be damned if he was going to pass up this opportunity.

He also knew that the old man had two ungodly beautiful twin daughters who would be heading to the barn in a little while. He had paid their Bible-thumping old father one of his gold teeth, half of what they agreed on. The old bearded man had assured him the girls would visit him in the barn before too long. The mother must have overheard, because she set to squawkin' until the old man gave her a backhand to the chops that shut her up. Mueller smiled at the memory. Reminded him of his own ma and pa.

The food had been decent enough, but the family was a gloomy bunch, as if someone had just died, which wasn't really his concern. The only thing he wanted right now was them twins. After they were all through, he was to pay them the other gold tooth, which they'd bring directly to their pa. It was all fine and dandy with Mueller, because he wasn't going to let the old man have the gold for long anyway. It couldn't work out any better, really.

The other thing he had learned, for certain, and the reason the old man was probably so sugar-sweet to him, was because he bet the old man planned on killing him for his gear and horses. Seemed like him and that big boy took a shine to his horses, kept asking questions, wanted to know all about them. What sort of gear he had, how many guns did he carry, that sort of thing.

Mueller had gladly told him whatever he figured the man wanted to hear, made it seem like he'd gladly sell him Slocum's horse. Sure, sure, anything you want, Mueller had hinted, we can come to a deal. But none of it would matter, as he would get it all back by morning, before moving on. Maybe even take along a twin or two, depending, of course, on how well they performed for him tonight.

And then, there they were, looking sheepish and scared and confused, all at once. They hadn't seen him yet, backed up as he was in the shadows of the stall he'd chosen to bed down in. He stepped into the honeyed glow of the lamplight.

"Howdy, girls. I am Tunk and we are about to have us the most fun you have ever had." Or ever will have again, he thought. Then he slid his big Bowie knife out of its sheath and, smiling, waggled a coil of rope. "Who's first?"

29

It was still dark, but not long before dawn, when Slocum felt something poking him in the arm. He came awake in an instant and snatched at the poking thing as his eyes snapped open.

Judith let out a yelp of surprise and ducked her head low. The poking thing had been her hand. "Sorry," she said, "but you didn't have to grab me like that."

"Why did you wake me?"

"Cause I swear I saw someone walking around down there."

"One of your family? Or was it Mueller?"

"I don't know, Mr. Slocum, I have never quite learned to see in the dark. Maybe it's something that comes with age?"

"Stop being a smart mouth." He looked into the graying dark toward the house. "How long was I asleep? It looks to be nearly dawn." The waning moonlight barely outlined the house and barn. As he watched, he fancied he could also make out the fence he'd rescued the men from days before.

"A couple of hours, I think. I dozed off a few times, but not for very long, I'm sure of it."

"Good, because that's when people tend to sneak up on you."

From below, they heard the sudden shouts of men, confused, perhaps, or startled from sleep. And another, louder voice, also

171

a man's, barking orders. It sounded to Slocum like Mueller. He got to his knees and peered into the gloom.

"What's going on down there, Mr. Slocum?" Judith whispered in his ear, looking down toward the dull light glowing from the ranch house's front windows.

He only had enough time to shake his head once, then a gunshot like a hand clap rang out, followed by another, then several seconds later a third shot echoed out. A woman's scream was quickly stifled, as if by a hand.

"Dammit! I shouldn't have slept so long. I have to get down there—got to be Mueller." Slocum rose and, snatching up his rifle, hobbled down the backside of the ledge-sided rise, tripping once over an unseen rock. He heard the gun stock smack against the rock and hoped it wasn't broken. He had a feeling he'd need it soon.

"You okay?" Judith was right behind him.

"Yeah, yeah. Look," he said over his shoulder, trying to keep as quiet as possible as they neared the base. "I need to keep quiet and get to the house. I want you to run down by the barn, around the back, try not to spook the animals. Rig up that wagon and saddle all the horses. Harness the team if you can. Then wait for me there, out of sight. But most important, keep alert and keep your head down. Mueller's a mean piece of work. If I can, I'll take care of him, then I'm going to use your father to find that arsenal he has in the barn."

She nodded. "I'm sure he has the key."

"Yeah, and if I can't get it, I'll just blast my way in, okay? Now go, but stay safe and keep hidden."

Before Mueller showed up, he'd intended to set up a distraction, then break into the house and get the women out, tie up the men, or shoot them if he needed to. Then haul the lot of them to Slaterville. But regardless of what he did with the men, he intended to get the women loaded into the wagon and headed toward that town. It wasn't the direction they wanted to go in, but they could at least get protection from the crazy old bastard there, before moving on. It wasn't much of a plan, he admitted, but it was better than leaving them to slowly die here under the thumb of that deranged zealot.

But that had all been before the killer arrived. Once Tunk wandered on in, Slocum had intended to deal with him first, in the barn. But sleep—his and Judith's—had blown holes in that plan. He low-walked across the road, cursing again the fact that he'd slept longer than he intended. He pointed at Judith, then motioned in the gray light toward the far end of the barn. "Wait there," he whispered.

She nodded, but he doubted like hell she'd listen to him. Hadn't yet. Not many strong-willed women did all that much listening, it seemed to him. And judging from how the old Bible-thumping Tinker treated his wife and girls, he was surprised it took her that long to work up the nerve to leave him. Though he bet she'd been gone, at least in her own head, for years. Just waiting for the right moment, as she'd said, to really leave.

He headed left, looking to skirt the end of the front fence, then cut in close to the low ranch house. An oil lamp, much like the previous night, glowed from the back of the house, nearby the kitchen.

He'd never counted on Mueller to show up. Never in a hundred years did he think the man would have actually turned around. He'd worked hard to make enemies of everyone he'd encountered. So why did the man come back? Slocum dashed to the side of the house, then bent low and listened at the plank wall.

He heard a woman sobbing, sounded like the old lady, then boot steps, and a man's voice, Mueller's, said, "What did I tell you? Shut your caterwauling, or I'll do for you what I did for him. Big bastard should have known better. I'm the one with the gun and he's the one with a permanent headache."

So, thought Slocum, the last of the sons, no doubt dead. He couldn't say that he was sorry. They hadn't been the most pleasant fellows to be around. And one Tinker male would make his job easier.

He had to see in there, had to know what was going on. He reached up with a hand and felt for a windowsill. There it was, just over his head to the left. It was still dark enough, and he wasn't backlit by rising sunlight since he was on the west end of the house. He rose slowly, until he was looking in through a corner of a wavy glass pane.

There was Mueller, still wearing that rank red shirt. Must be ripe by now, thought Slocum. The killer stood in the door-way to the room, talking low and running the tip of his rifle barrel along Ruth's neck and shoulders. It was difficult for Slocum to see, but it looked as if Ruth's face had been welted up. By the old man, his son, or Mueller? It hardly mattered now.

The old woman sat on the floor closer to the window; he only saw her head, rocking back and forth, but he saw the body of the older boy, Zeke, laid out on the floor, unmoving. Slocum assumed she was cradling her son's head. She had a kerchief wrapped tight around her own mouth, no doubt because she'd cried out in her grief, and for it she had incited the killer's promised wrath. Slocum toyed with the idea of poking his rifle through the glass and shooting Mueller, but there were too many things that could go wrong. What if he missed? He didn't know where the rest of them were. The old man's whereabouts didn't bother him so much, but the children? The twins? In a house this small, there might well be other people behind Mueller. Or Mueller could accidentally jerk his trigger, shoot Ruth or another person in the room.

He dropped back down, slowly so his movement didn't draw attention, then low-walked around the back corner of the house. If he could get inside, he could get the drop on Mueller, force him out. Then deal with the Tinker family mess later. But first things first . . .

Slocum stepped onto the back porch. He paused dead in front of the back door, faint lamplight leaking through gaps in the boards. He risked a quick glance to his left, then right. No one in sight. He looked again toward the direction of the barn. He hoped Judith hadn't found any trouble. He was relieved when he saw Mueller in the house, knowing Judith would be out of harm's way.

Slocum stepped quickly to the side of the door. It looked rigid, though it might give in under one quick kick. But that would alert Mueller and give him time to duck out of the way.

He tried the wooden drop latch, found it to be locked, then he heard the killer's voice again.

"Shut up that Bible mumbo-jumbo, old man. I tied you up, but damn, I can just as surely shoot you. I need some bargaining power, but I don't need but one person to use as leverage against that damn Slocum. I know he's around here somewheres. Which one of you is going to fess up as to his whereabouts?"

So that was it. The man knew who he was, not a big effort on Mueller's part. He must have seen Slocum, and figured it out when he'd shot him in the leg. If not, then he'd certainly recognized the Appaloosa, and no doubt firmed up the guess when he found his traps and rifled his belongings. He had a couple items that bore his name tucked way down in the saddle bags.

And then Slocum thought of the folded-up wanted poster. Mueller would have found that, too, and would know that Slocum knew he was wanted for other crimes elsewhere. And that Mueller might not be his real name.

"I get him off my back, then you and me, girly, we're going to have some fun."

Slocum heard Ruth's low voice say something, though he couldn't make it out. But it must have angered Mueller, for he heard a hard sound, like a slap. She didn't cry out. He would have been surprised if she had. Tough woman. He hoped she wasn't so tough that she was going to keep on mouthing off to him. Another thing Judith shared with her.

"You like that, do you? Like it when a man gets rough with you?" He slapped her again. "Pretty or no, you'll get to like a few other things I got in store for you."

Mueller's laugh was the last straw.

Slocum stepped back, let loose with a hard heel kick. The wooden latch splintered and the door flew inward. A board hung askew before him. Slocum shoved it out of his way and didn't waste any time barreling into the house. Even as he did, Mueller spun on him.

Slocum pulled the trigger at the same time the killer did. He barely avoided the blast from Tunk's rifle, then he heard a slam. Smoke filled the air and Slocum found himself staring at the closed door of the room Mueller had everyone locked up in.

He heard more cries of surprise from the children inside. What a lousy few days they've had. Hell, thought Slocum, what lousy lives. But then to top it all off with Tunk Mueller tying them up, shooting their uncle, smacking their grandparents and mother?

Slocum didn't think his bullet hit Mueller, and he hoped no one else got it. From what he remembered in looking in the window, no one had been directly across from Tunk.

The house smelled of gun smoke and, behind it, stagnant night air, the tang of a cold wood fire, and stale cooking smells.

"Glad to see you could make the event of the year, Slocum. Now, I want you to hold your fire, because when I open this door, there's going to be one pretty little lady in front of me, and we wouldn't want you to shoot her, right?"

Slocum licked his lips. Think, think, he told himself. "Tunk, you leave her out of this. Come on out here and fight me like a man."

He heard Tunk laughing. "Someone should have drowned you at birth, Slocum. You're a real disappointment to me. I have no desire to fight you at all. I want you to put down your gun so this lady don't get hurt. Nor these children. Now, when I open this door, you are going to come into this room, no guns in your hands, or I will shoot one person at a time. It might take a while, since this appears to be a nest of breeders, but I'll get it done."

That time, Slocum did hear Ruth gasp. The mother in her wasn't nearly as tough as the angry woman who endured the slaps of men.

Seconds passed. The notion of giving up his guns forced Slocum to grind his teeth together hard. He weighed the risks of kicking in this door, too. With that red shirt as a guide, he could drill a shot or two from his Colt into Mueller before the foul piece of trash knew what happened.

And then a child sobbed and the decision was made for him.

"I'll come in, Mueller, but don't you dare hurt anyone!" He

set down the rifle and pistol, handles facing the room, hoping that might make it easier to grab for them if the situation arose.

"I will dare to do anything I damn well please, and don't you forget it." As if to prove his point, he heard Ruth shout and a scuffle of some sort ensued. "Get down, woman! Or next time I will cave in your head!" Then he shouted, "Hands high, Slocum, and don't do anything you shouldn't or I will snuff out another of these here God-fearing people, so help me!"

Slocum thought the killer was starting to sound a little nervous. Good. He turned to the side, trying to keep himself as narrow a target as possible, and lifted the wooden latch. The door swung inward with a slow squeak and he saw the room and its inhabitants. The window through which he'd peeked showed more gray light.

The room was a bedroom, with several rope beds and straw-filled mattresses slashed and strewn, the prickly dried grasses poking from the slashed rents as if they were the guts of some mythical animal.

On the floor, before the window, sat the old woman, trussed with rope, the kerchief tied around her mouth, her son's head in her lap. She could not hold him with her arms, tied to her sides as they were, but she cradled his bloodied head, her own nightgown a sopping, blood-matted thing. She appeared to be oblivious to the foul situation around her as she rocked slowly back and forth over her dead son.

Along the other side of the room, children lay huddled in a corner, the older ones crouched around the younger, protecting them, looking outward with wild animal eyes. They will never be the same after this, thought Slocum. Even what they had was better than this.

Far from them, in the other corner, crouched the old man, also trussed with rope. Nevertheless in his lap lay his Bible, or what was left of the leather-bound tome. It had been savaged, ripped apart, pages scattered about the room. His gray beard was streaked with blood from a gash on the side of his bald head. Slocum thought he saw the gleam of bone as the blood flowed.

The old man blinked, and his head trembled side to side as

if he were an old palsy victim. A bad enough head knock was something people often didn't recover from, and judging from the dazed expression on the old man's face, the distant look in his glassy eyes, and the wobble of his head, he was well out of it. Still, he seemed to be moving his lips. Praying, maybe. Hope it helps, thought Slocum.

Where were the twins? He had a strange feeling that Mueller knew, maybe had already dealt with them. He'd have to worry about them later.

In the middle of the room, Ruth stood, looking frightened and angry at the same time, tied tightly but sloppily with rope crisscrossing her body, her nightgown cinched tight to her body, her breasts painfully lashed with ropes. The top of her nightgown had been torn, so that one bare shoulder was revealed. Her face bore purple and yellow bruises, but Slocum assumed her father had done that to her. They were too old-looking to have come from Mueller.

Then she met Slocum's eyes with a hard gaze that cut to the knot of children then back to him, and told him all he suspected: Do whatever you have to, she seemed to be saying, but don't let him harm the children.

Mueller had a pistol rammed against the side of Ruth's head. His arm was tight around her neck, a scaly elbow poking through a hole in the red shirt. He peeked around her face, and as if to emphasize his position of superiority in the situation, he jerked his arm tight, causing her to gag. He smiled while he did it, jamming the barrel tip of his pistol harder against her temple.

"All right, Mueller." Slocum stepped into the room, hands high. "Beating up a house full of old people and women and children doesn't exactly make you a tough hombre in my book. You want me, you got me. Leave these people alone and let's settle this thing outdoors, just the two of us. You want me dead and I want you dead. Let's end it now."

"Not another step, Slocum!" Even as he said it, Tunk stepped backward one step closer to the window. The killer's nostrils flexed with his hard breathing. Slocum saw loose strands of

Ruth's hair caught in the man's mouth, others moved with his breath. Mueller's eyes were tinged with a whole lot more crazy than Old Man Tinker's had been.

Slocum looked into Ruth's eyes, then glanced hard at the window, back to her, then to the window. She blinked slowly once. It was now or never. Slocum had to get the pistol away from Ruth's head as he moved forward, but there wasn't a damn thing he could do. Ruth had to do it all, and as Slocum ducked and drove forward, reaching to push away the pistol, Ruth jerked her head forward and drove backward with her entire body.

At the same time, Slocum moved in close, slashed downward, and knocked Tunk's gun hand down and away. The killer didn't drop his gun, but it didn't matter. Once Ruth set him moving toward the window, the old woman flopped flat on her back and Tunk stepped right on her, lost his footing, and Ruth kept pushing, even as Slocum snatched at her, grabbing the ropes and a handful of nightgown. It tore but he held on and Tunk Mueller kept going, folding up and collapsing through the window.

Slocum pushed Ruth down onto a ravaged straw mattress and tore out of the room, snatching up his Colt and rifle on the run. He hit the door casing hard and used the little back porch to propel himself toward the corner of the house, keeping low. As he ran straight out and angled past the corner of the house, cocking his guns, he had expected to see a stunned Tunk Mueller lying on his back on the ground.

But the only thing he saw was a mess of glass and wood. He advanced and kept his gaze locked on the front corner of the house. He glanced down quickly once and saw the unmistakable spatter of blood. Mueller was bleeding, and from the look of the trail of it, he'd taken a lot of glass to the back.

Slocum, back tight to the house, advanced to the front corner. He peeked around once and was rewarded with a bullet nicking the wood a foot above his head.

Mueller was not too cut up to shoot. Slocum looked at the ground again. But the man was definitely cut up. He bent low and risked another peek, saw Mueller stumbling for the barn. "Oh no you don't, you son of a bitch," Slocum swore as he ran, then pulled up.

"Mueller! I got you dead to rights! Drop that pistol and turn around now!"

Tunk was halfway to the barn. He stopped, raised his arms, his pistol still held in one bleeding hand. Slocum advanced slowly, holstered his Colt, and kept the rifle trained on the red shirt, now sodden with blood and jagged hunks of glass poking from it. The back of the man's head was matted with blood.

"I said, drop that gun and turn around! Now!"

Mueller's head leaned to one side. Slocum recognized that cocky pose and wanted to just shoot the man and be done with it. But he'd made a habit of not shooting people in the back, and he wasn't about to let a murderer like Mueller break that trend.

Tunk started to turn, still holding the pistol. Slocum knew that meant the killer was going to force the play. "Fine by me," muttered Slocum, angling sideways. And then he saw movement from the barn, beyond Mueller. Judith stepped out, hands by her sides.

"You bastard!" she shouted.

Slocum barked, "Judith, no! Get out of there!"

Mueller faced her. "Who in the hell are you?" He cocked the pistol, and before Slocum could get off a shot, he heard two shots almost on top of each other. As the smoke cleared, he saw Mueller still standing, but weaving, his back considerably more bloody and ragged than it had been seconds before. Beyond him, Judith stood, her six-guns in her hands, curls of smoke rising from the barrels. "For the twins," she said, and holstered her guns.

Mueller looked down at his gut, said, "You little bitch . . ." As he raised his pistol again, Slocum cored his head with a rifle shot. Tunk Mueller pitched forward, facedown in the dirt.

For a moment, no one moved. Then Slocum walked toward Judith. "What the hell were you thinking? He could have killed you."

She did not smile. "I don't think so, Mr. Slocum. I told you I knew how to use them."

"Yeah," he said. "I guess you do at that." He looked past her at the barn. He hated to ask, but he had to know. "The twins?"

Her face sagged into grief and she shook her head. "I gave him one for each of them. What he did to them . . . it ain't right. I should have been there, could have helped them."

He held her shoulders. "No, Judith. If you had been here, he would have . . ."

She leaned into him and wept, and all he could do was hold her and let her cry.

30

"Think you'll be back this way anytime soon?" Ruth stood by the Appaloosa, stroking its neck, not looking at Slocum. He touched her chin and she looked up at him, trying to smile.

"There will be at least one bounty on him, maybe two." He nodded toward the canvas-and-rope-wrapped body draped and tied over the mule. "I'll leave him and your mule in Slaterville and make sure that the reward money gets to you. It will be enough to get you to California and begin a life there besides."

"You could bring it yourself." Ruth's eyes widened.

"I could . . . but I have someplace to go, some friends I want to visit. A ranching couple and their foreman. I wasn't able to say good-bye properly before I left, and I feel badly about that."

She lowered her head, nodded. "Thank you for leaving that fine horse for Judith." She looked toward the front gate, where Judith stood, staring southward, her back to them. "She will have need of a good horse. Something to carry her to places none of us may ever see."

"Judith will get there. This is only an interruption. You all are strong women. You'll get to where you want to be. I can tell." He raised Ruth's face again and kissed her lightly. "Are you sure you'll be okay? I can bury Mueller here and stay on awhile, help you get righted around."

She squared her shoulders and smiled at him. "Don't you worry your pretty head over us, Mr. Slocum. We are, as you say, strong women and made of tough stuff. And besides, every man I've ever met has brought nothing but trouble with him. Off with you."

He kissed her again, hard this time. She kissed him back, then pushed him away. "Off, I said. Before I change my opinion of men . . . John."

He walked the horse and mule to the front fence, the fence where so much had occurred, and stopped at the gate. Judith, looking fresh as a spring daisy, save for her red-rimmed eyes, stood waiting for him. About her waist rode her six-shooters, oiled and holstered.

She had never looked more like a child and a woman to him, all at once, than at that moment. Someday, Slocum thought, someday soon, Judith, you will make men weep and vow to the moon and the sun anything for you. If I were a younger man and wasn't always on the run, I'd be one of them.

"Mr. Slocum," she said in a very businesslike tone, "I have given the matter much thought." Her eyes locked with his, then looked down again. "And I will accompany you on your travels. It is only right. I am, after all, the one who shot this foul creature." She nodded toward the dead bundle on the mule.

"Yes, you shot him, Judith." Slocum tried not to smile. "But I believe it was my shot that killed him. Don't forget that. It is important. Shooting someone and taking their life are two different things, after all. And you are too young to have killed someone."

And then she broke, as he'd hoped she would, and collapsed against him, much as she had done the day before. "I . . . I can't stay here, Mr. Slocum. I can't, I just can't."

"Ruth needs you, Judith. Just for a time. She has a lot to figure out. Your parents are not well. Your mother will heal, in time. Your father, though, I fear, will not. He is addled and is losing ground. I don't say this to scare you, but you should know what you face."

"I am not afraid of that. As long as Ruth and Mama and the children are all right, we will muddle through. I know that."

She looked up at him. "But I need to see the world, Mr. Slocum. I cannot stay here. Something inside me is telling me I have things to do, people to see, places to go. Isn't that how you feel? You said yourself those were things you needed to do."

She looked so hopeful to him. He sighed. "I know, Judith. Believe me, I know. I don't suppose it will help you to hear that we all go through what you are feeling. Every blessed one of us."

She looked up at him, her eyes welling. She shook her head, and he kissed her forehead and hugged her. "Just don't be in such a rush. There's plenty of time for happiness, once you find the right person."

"What if I already found him?" She looked at him, searching, he knew, for some sign from him, for something he could not give her.

"Then you'll both know. Trust me, Judith. You'll both know it."

He mounted up, urged the Appaloosa, leading the mule and the dead man, south to Slaterville. From there, he would ride southeast to Arizona, and the little graveyard on the knoll at the Rocking D. To visit some friends.